If he kissed her again
the madness might recur

"Trudi Carr, I'm in love with you. Will you marry me?"

"Stop joking about things like that, Dan Johnson!" Trudi moved away, determined to fight the insane desire to love him. "It must be the moonlight. Tomorrow we'll have forgotten all this nonsense."

He cradled her lovingly, completely the master. "Don't fight me, Trudi. Will you marry me?" His voice was low and his eyes serious.

Trudi gasped, realizing that Dan had deliberately repeated the question. "You hardly know me! I told you, I'm a career girl. I'm not interested in love and marriage."

"But that was before you knew me. You can't resist me, Trudi, even if you wanted to."

"You're crazy," she murmured against his mouth. "But if it's any consolation, I'm crazy too."

The Man from Ti Kouka

Rosalie Henaghan

Harlequin Books

TORONTO • NEW YORK • LONDON
AMSTERDAM • PARIS • SYDNEY • HAMBURG
STOCKHOLM • ATHENS • TOKYO • MILAN

Original hardcover edition published in 1982
by Mills & Boon Limited

ISBN 0-373-02572-6

Harlequin Romance first edition September 1983

For my mother

Printed in U.S.A.

CHAPTER ONE

'AT last—Ti Kouka turn off!'

'Oh no, a shingle road! In this heat that's all we needed!' Trudi, a slim brown-haired girl at the wheel of the late model car, sighed. 'I was beginning to think Ti Kouka had joined the realms of fantasy.'

'Some dream, a stone mansion on one of the richest farms in the country! I wonder if we'll be able to see much of it from the campsite.' The younger girl twisted her shiny gold wedding band absently. 'John told me it has some interesting pioneering relics.'

'From the heat and the dust, Maria, I'll be a relic before we get anywhere near the place!'

'Trudi, let's stop. There's a stream under those trees just ahead.'

The driver, shading her eyes from the white glare of the road, pulled under the green of the overhanging willows. For a moment there was just the faint gurgle of the stream, then as the coolness penetrated both girls opened their doors.

'Lovely!' sighed Trudi in tones of relief. She eased her body from the seat, ungluing herself from the upholstery. 'Maria, there's a pool formed by the culvert that's big enough to soak in!'

Without pausing to change the girl slipped into the pool. Her hair turned into thick black strands around her pale face, making the dark-fringed eyes look darker and larger. The smile of bliss as she entered the water hid the determined little chin but not the softness of her mouth.

'Hurry up, Maria. This is lovely! At last I feel as if I'm on holiday. What a shame you've only two days away from that man of yours.'

'You wait till you're married, Trudi. John would let me have longer, but I don't want to be away from him.'

'Love!' snorted her older sister, standing up in the pool and brushing the water from her eyes. 'What's it done to you? Landed you with a husband who gets transferred three months after you're married, and you can't even get a position as a barrister, because you might be shifted again in a few months, or a few days, or a few years!'

'That's not accurate and you know it!' Maria shot back, but her stricken face told how the hit had reached home. 'I love John, we're very happy. At least at home I'm keeping up my research, and I'm confident John will get the next long-term position. I'll soon be working again.'

'I suppose I should be glad the perfect male's taken off to Wellington for these two days. At least I owe him that.' Trudi looked at her sister's disconsolate face and realised she had hurt her. Immediately she splashed over to her sister. 'Maria, I'm sorry, I'm a beast about your John. I would have been the same about any man, no matter how marvellous, if he ruined your career. But if you're happy then that's all that matters. Don't take any notice of me, I'm just an old maid who's anti men.'

Maria looked at her with a trace of a smile.

'I love John, Trudi. One day when you fall in love you'll understand!'

'But you were doing so well!' Trudi expostulated. She saw her sister's stormy face and began to chuckle as she realised what she had done.

'I'm like a dog with a bone! I just can't leave it alone. Here I'll dig a little hole in the pool and bury it right now and promise faithfully never to dig it up.' She stood like a statue in the pool and addressed her reflection. 'Prisoner at the pool, do you solemnly swear to leave the subject alone?' 'Yes, your honour,' she mimicked her answer gaily.

Seeing Maria's face was smiling again, Trudi flicked water at her recumbent figure. Maria retaliated, then ordered a stay in proceedings until she had placed the drink bottle from the car into the pool. Then the splashing resumed. With much yelling and shouting the two continued until Maria sought the sanctuary of the bank and Trudi declared herself the victor of the pool stakes. She laughed as she gazed ruefully at herself. She was soaked from head to foot and her top was clinging to her. It was just as well none of the staff could see her now, she mused. They wouldn't have recognised the usually sophisticated figure of Miss Trudi Carr, Production Manager of Maugh's Fashions, and the Court would hardly approve the apparel of her sister, Mrs John Benton, as suitable for a rising young barrister. She looked at her sister fondly.

Maria was very like her, but she had a softer gamine appeal which seemed emphasised by the short cap of dark curls. Her femininity was obvious and it was part of her personality that Maria was instantly liked by all who met her. Her charm hid, too, a brain that was coolly analytical, except where her beloved husband was concerned. Even to herself, Trudi had to admit that her sister had never looked prettier or happier in her life. Quite obviously marriage suited her well.

The ripples on the pool had settled and Trudi glanced down catching sight, Narcissus-like, of herself, a pale wraith with widely spaced, all-seeing sombre dark eyes that lost themselves in the hazel brown base of the pool. She grinned at herself cheerfully and kicked the pool into action, and the reflection smiled briefly back at her before dissolving into a thousand pieces. With a scoop of her arm she flung a stream of diamond-lit drops which dazzled briefly in an arc, before plopping into the water downstream.

At the same time she became aware of the figure. He sat his horse as though he owned the world, an unconscious arrogance that made Trudi lift her own head proudly to meet his eyes. She couldn't mistake his smiling admiration, but at her stare his expression changed. Discomfited, she looked away and her eyes lit on the bottle. She fished it out composedly, clambered as best she could out on to the bank and calmly poured out the drink as though she was sitting sedately at her afternoon tea table.

'Excuse me, I didn't want to spoil your fun.'

Trudi looked at the man coolly. 'We've finished.'

Calmly she handed the mug to Maria, who had sat up at the stranger's voice and was now smiling openly at him. The man had swung down easily in a smooth graceful movement and led the horse to the creek, downstream from where they sat.

'Would you like a drink? It's still warm, but it's better than it was, thanks to the pool.' Maria's voice was apologetic as she held out the full mug of orange.

'Thank you.' His voice was deep and he took the mug and drained it quickly. 'Where are you making for?'

'That's of no concern to you.'

Trudi spoke softly but firmly. She was aware of the quick smile that spread over the stranger's face as he looked at her. Trudi became instantly aware of the long tassels of thick wet hair, her shirt clinging curvaceously to her body and the speculative gleam in the stranger's eyes, as he assessed her long legs and the brief shorts she wore. If only she had been seen by this odious man in a slightly less undignified state, she thought bitterly. She knew he was finding the whole scene one of considerable mirth, and if she had known him better she could have laughed at herself too. With an over-played attempt at a straight face he handed back the mug deliberately to her and she knew he was thinking that she was the rude mug in question. For Maria he smiled dazzlingly before turning to his horse.

'Had enough, feller? Come on.'

He spoke softly to the horse as he rubbed its neck while the creature lifted its velvet mouth and nuzzled him affectionately. Again with an easy vault he was astride and then with a casual wave he had left, riding sedately past the screen of the trees.

'That's a real thirst-quencher, Trudi.' Maria was at last having a drink. 'Couldn't let that poor man go thirsty in this heat when we have so much. Wasn't he devastating? I always did like tall strong men with black hair and deep brown eyes. How I fell in love with my darling short blond John is still a mystery!' she chuckled. 'Our visitor was a real hunk of mas-culinity.'

'And he's probably got some poor woman who runs around after him like a slave! Hrmph! Some silly wench who thinks just because he whispered "I love you" she can throw up her own career to cook and clean and. . . .' She broke off, seeing the look in Maria's eye. 'Sorry, sorry, sorry! Peace, Maria!'

Lying back on the bank, she closed her eyes against the glare of the sun to allow it to dry her clothes and hair before getting back into the car. She had to admit that Maria had been accurate. The man was physically attractive. Even in those few moments he had shown a sense of humour, as well as pride, and he had cared for the horse, stroking it sensitively, which showed he had a gentle side to him. Still, the way he had seemed to expect the rapid offering of the drink, before Maria had even slaked her own thirst, proved that he considered himself as one of God's gifts to women. His smile at Maria had been full of charm, but the long challenging look he had given herself had been maddening. Obviously he was one of the dangerous ones, she told herself, a man to be avoided by any young woman of sense. It was just as well that their paths would not cross.

Conscious of a vague irritation, she packed up the drink and mugs neatly, then pulled Maria up.

'Let's get going, Sis.'

She didn't want to admit that the wretched man had upset the even tenor of her day, evaporating all the joyful expectancy of her two-day break. When she had first heard about the campsite at Ti Kouka's Bell Bay from a friend she had been in the thick of winter orders. The heavy tweeds and leathers had made the sound of sea, sand and bush sound like heaven. Best of all had been the fact that it was very private, being owned by the Ti-Kouka estate who kept it as a camping ground for their own friends. She had written to make enquiries and had received a detailed letter back stating dryly that the facilities were limited to cold water showers and toilets in a bare paddock. Obviously they were not wanting additional business. The letter had delighted her. Such isolation was just what she wanted—peace, quiet and not a telephone for miles.

A neighbour had loaned them a tent and they had been shown how to erect it; modern materials had made it simple. Tales of difficulty Trudi had laughed away.

It was typical, she supposed, of man's need to brag, to make fools of women who were quite capable of managing alone. Types like that 'hunk', as Maria had called him. She pursed her mouth firmly and combed her hair, relaxing into a grin when she saw the look on her face.

'I've been looking at the letter. According to my calculations we must be close to Ti Kouka. I don't suppose we'll see much of it from the road at any rate, more's the pity.'

'The farm's been handed down in the same family from the first surveying of the land. One of the few estates that haven't been hacked to pieces over the years,' Maria commented.

'Well, we might be able to glimpse a little, seeing they mentioned that the camp was only a kilometre from the homestead.'

Trudi eased the car out on the road. The dust which seeped in didn't seem quite so bad as it had been before their halt.

Now relaxed and cooler, Trudi drove steadily, as the stones formed ridges in the road. Within a minute they had entered a valley and the countryside had undergone a change. She noticed the richness of the fields and the lushness of the pasture that was totally different from the dry hills. Easing down a steep turn, she paused instinctively.

'Look at that!'

Even without Maria's gasp of admiration she pulled over and stopped. Massive trees enclosed a park-like lawn which led up to a grey stone house, its many large windows glinting in the sun. From where they sat the view was partly obscured by a band of trees, but there was no mistaking the grandeur of the property.

'It's fabulous,' admired Trudi sincerely. 'Just the sort of mansion I'd love to call home.' She turned to her sister with a grin. 'A bit different from my current abode!'

'Imagine living there! They would have terrific views over this valley and straight through the gap to the sea. Look, the sea, the sea! Let's get cracking. A proper swim would be gorgeous.'

Trudi pulled out again and shortly passed the drive which led towards the now hidden house. The road deteriorated sharply and all her concentration was focused on to the rutted track that was all that remained.

Beside her lay the sea and on the other side the steep hills. The scenery was magnificent, but she had little chance to appreciate it as she was concentrating on her car's movements. A minute later the track levelled and she pulled over to look around her.

The sense of isolation pleased her. They might have been alone in a primeval world. It was majestic country, the sleeping giants of the hills, covered in the greens of the bush, reaching to the sea. The waves pounded down ferociously, as though angry with the silent hills, and the rocks, white and black, stood like an advanced guard across the sand. The waves, blue-green, crested, and smashed in white foam, retreated, then gathered force to try again, crashing on to the strange rocks in some ceaseless rhythm.

The road led round a curve and the track opened into a paddock, where a couple of brightly coloured tents and two caravans announced that they had reached their destination. Two children looked up at their arrival, then scampered off towards the beach. In the centre of the paddock a line of trees formed a natural division. Someone had pitched a tent under the cliffs and looking out to sea. Two caravans were parked side by side and beside them was a jeep and a trailer loaded with a small boat.

'What about over on the other side?' pointed Maria. 'There's a small rise which would protect us from any southerly likely to spring up and we could look straight out to the sea and the cliffs.'

'And it's nice and private,' commented Trudi.

A few moments later they were gazing round with delight at the crescent of the ground shaped by the line of bush-covered hills leading to the steep white cliffs which formed such a landmark. A small curve in the line of the shore meant that further down the force of the waves was not so strong, although the beach immediately in front of them was littered with driftwood like the bones of a drowned forest.

'Someone may have just moved away from this site. Look, it really is a beauty—there's a natural fireplace with those stones, someone must have lugged them there. One thing we don't have to worry about is firewood.' Maria looked around again. 'We're a long way from the toilets and showers, though.'

'That's just as well, Maria. From what I've heard of those sort of places at camping grounds, it's wise not to be too close!'

They both laughed and together they began positioning the tent.

The small bag it fitted into was light and while Maria carried the bag, Trudi began unfolding the material. They made swift work of it, tightening the cords on to the metal pegs. When the main ones were in at an angle they secured the smaller pegs, then adjusted them so that the tent stood taut. Over it went the bright orange fly cover that would protect them in the event of rain.

It was simplicity itself to fit, and the front long cord Trudi fastened to a handy fence-post as a clothes line. Proprietorially they ran inside, giggling with success like a pair of teenagers again. They began unloading the car, putting in additional groundsheets to fit the floor of the tent and then the broad thick piece of foam which fitted the area to provide a comfortable base for the sleeping bags or as a seat. Under the protection of the orange cover but outside the tent Trudi placed the large box and the foam chilli-bin for the food.

With most of the car unpacked they felt quite pleased with their effort, and Trudi offered to make their first cup of tea. Instead of utilising the small stove they had purchased, the girls decided to light a fire to try out their skills. To their joy the large barbecue grill they brought with them fitted over the fireplace exactly, and while Maria went towards the tap with an empty bucket for water, Trudi gathered driftwood from the beach. Some of the shapes were so peculiar she instinctively found herself imagining birds and trees and space fiction characters. Smiling at the thoughts, she took the pile back and soon had a fire glowing.

'I do wish John could see this spot,' said Maria. 'Isn't it heavenly? Tomorrow let's explore those hills. Look at those cabbage trees on the top of those cliffs. They look just like a warrior's top knot.'

Trudi smiled, agreeing to the aptness of the description. 'All right, but I'm voting for the beach now. By the way, you didn't tell me just why John had to fly up to Wellington?'

'I don't know. It's a surprise,' Maria said equably.

Trudi was flabbergasted. That her sister's husband should calmly leave his wife for two days while he flitted off on a pleasure trip staggered her. Her face must have said volumes, for Maria burst out laughing.

'Darling, he's not Bluebeard!' she chuckled. 'His boss asked him to check with the Wellington section of the company, so it's partly work. He's quite the white-haired boy since he pulled off those two deals which were hanging fire before. But there's another reason. You remember those lovely deep blue pottery bowls we were given as a wedding present? The potter lived in Wellington, and I feel sure John's gone to fetch a big vase for an anniversary present. In three weeks we'll have been married for a year.'

'Goodness, I hadn't realised,' Trudi frowned. She should have made a note in her diary earlier in the year to mark her sister's anniversary. After all, she had been her sister's bridesmaid on that occasion.

'It's slipped my mind. Would you like a new suit or dress or something else?'

'I'd love a new outfit, Trudi. Since I've stopped earning I've had to be very economy-minded. We want to save for a house of our own.'

'It was a pity John had to take up the transfer to Ashburton so soon after your marriage,' commented Trudi. 'You really loved working, and your boss was so disappointed.'

Too late she saw the trap, but for once Maria didn't seem to notice, but spoke thoughtfully. 'I do miss it. When I was working I found the reality is decidedly unglamorous. The research side is far more interesting and I was really enjoying that. Since I've been at home I've been able to follow my own inclinations and I've learnt a lot. On the other hand there's nothing like the stimulation of having a specific case, and doing a job well. But when I see John's face light up on just seeing me, I'm getting paid, Trudi, far more than ever before.' Maria replaced her cup carefully and looked at her sister. 'It's true, although I know to you it might sound crazy. Of course, I'd like to go back to work, but in the meantime John's happy and so am I. John's transfer won't take for ever.'

Trudi nodded, admitting defeat. 'What colour does John like you in?'

'Trudi, you are a darling! Blue, particularly pale blue.' Maria's pleasure was so sincere that Trudi realised her hostility to the loss of her career had really worried her sister.

'One blue outfit coming up!' she smiled. 'C'mon, let's get to that big blue bath!'

It wasn't long before they were in their swimsuits and racing in long-legged strides towards the waves. They had to keep jumping the pieces of wood in their path and when they reached the beach, they darted in and out of the waves, as they went towards the sheltered curve of the bay. Halfway along they reached a large rock formation and stared at it in surprise.

'It looks like a giant carving of a Maori chief, a Rangitira—look, even the whorls of the tattoo are grooved on his face.'

The Rangitira appeared to ignore them, staring arrogantly out to sea. Trudi gazed at him and for an odd moment the chief's face seemed to dissolve and take on the aspect of the stranger who had appeared so disturbingly at the creek. The sun's rays struck at the same time, casting a golden glow about the rocks. She blinked and shook her head, telling herself to stop being fanciful. Maria had run on ahead and Trudi raced to catch her sister.

The beach took a sudden curve before curling to the feet of the steep white cliffs of limestone which blocked any further progress. The small bay was occupied by some of their fellow campers and they waved to them before swimming. The water was cool and relaxing.

Maria left the water first and lay spread on the golden sand while Trudi played raindrops with the waves until the memory of the pool and the man on the horse returned. Hastily she swam back to the beach and joined Maria. She felt herself under scrutiny and glanced up. High on the top of the cliffs above them stood a tall figure, a horse beside him, and instinctively she draped her towel around her.

'He must have wings!' she muttered, suddenly certain of the figure's identity.

'Need them with limestone,' put in Maria, her own gaze following Trudi's. 'You couldn't climb those cliffs. Look, further along towards the camp, the trees have a small gap in the bush, I bet there's a track through there.'

Studying it, Trudi nodded. There was a logical explanation, she reminded herself, for his apparent omnipresence. The high point would give a commanding view of Ti-Kouka's fields as well as their bathing spot. She knew a definite irritation that such a man should be observing them.

'Come on, let's go back to the tent.'

As they made their way into the camp they saw a small stile which led into a path heading towards the bush, and Maria suggested they explore the hill in the morning.

'In the meantime, I seem to have developed a tremendous appetite. It must be the clean, fresh air,' Trudi chuckled.

'We should take some more driftwood as we go.'

They made their way back to the tent and built a roaring fire, and amid much laughter they soon discovered it was not the way to cook. After the flames had lowered they cooked quite satisfactorily, the chops sizzling and the potatoes soon bubbling.

Aware that the evening was at last getting cooler, they changed and found that experience almost impossible in the confines of the tent. Amidst great hilarity they suddenly smelt the odour of burnt chops and the frizzled remains convinced them there was a lot to be said for electricity and controlled heat. The salad was easily fixed and the tomatoes and corn still made a nourishing meal. Trudi had to admit that the chops would have been delicious. Maria's comment that they were super burnt made them both chuckle.

Afterwards they lay back talking desultorily about mutual friends and new plans. Casting her eye around, Maria found a plank sitting by the fence and she propped it on two big stones. It too contributed to the merriment as she introduced the 'latest in lounge furniture'.

Other camp fires were being lit and the occupants of the tents and caravans were homing to the camping ground. The fire was almost dying down when both of them wondered about washing the dishes.

'I'll go. The tap's close to the other caravan, I might say hello to the folks there.' Maria spoke eagerly.

Trudi watched Maria dart off. The solitude which had such an appeal for her held no such joy for Maria. She moved to the car and pulled out her light jacket, one of their latest range. In the pocket was her usual notepad and pencil and she began sketching a dress for Maria. It was a simple style with an accent on draping over the shoulder, layer upon layer like the waves of the sea, swishing out into fullness at the waist. They had the perfect fabric for it in stock. She put the sketch away as Maria approached and threw a log on the fire.

'Thought you were letting the fire go out!'

'I nearly did,' apologised Trudi.

'Such a nice family in the caravan by the water tap,'

Maria reported. 'The man used to work on Ti Kouka and he brings his family every holidays. They say the fishing is superb.'

'Do you know, the water's boiling already,' put in Trudi with surprise. Despite the growing darkness the hiss of the bubbles could not be mistaken. 'Where did I put the detergent?'

'I just tripped on it! I have the feeling we should set aside one area for preparation!' laughed Maria. 'Look at the stars starting to shine, the air is so clear. I know I'm going to sleep like a log!'

'At least it's still warm, and the sleeping bags shouldn't be too hard on the base. It's certainly different from home. No bench to wipe down here,' Trudi chuckled, as she finished.

'The sea is very soothing, don't you think? Singing its own special lullaby. I wish my John was here with us. He'd really enjoy it.'

'Like the hunk.' Trudi spoke spontaneously, thinking of the stance of the figure on the cliff. She could have bitten her tongue at her sister's look.

'There's hope for you yet,' teased Maria. 'I thought you didn't approve!'

'I'm going to bed,' announced Trudi, glad that her expression was hidden by the darkness of the night.

Both girls took some time to settle.

'This reminds me of our last holiday with Dad,' put in Maria sleepily. 'I can still see him picking up a shell and making up stories about the pearl that lost its way.'

'That was a lovely tale,' Trudi said quietly. 'We were lucky. He was so good with stories. He was wonderful, the way he could spellbind.'

'Part of being a topline barrister,' said Maria. 'Sometimes I wonder if I'll ever be in the same class.'

'He always said you'd make a good lawyer.' Trudi didn't add that her father had always said that she had the makings of a barrister too. That dream had come to grief when she was seventeen. Their father had died when she was twelve and his loss had darkened her life.

Maria stirred, settling into the sleeping bag like a curled-up cat. Trudi lay back, then shot up when the tent fly gave a sudden crack. Realising it was only the effect of the wind, she lay down again, but sleep seemed far away. Again the fly cracked and she began to worry that the ignominy of having the tent collapse might be real. She had a momentary vision of the hunk standing by as she extricated herself from the heap. She could just imagine the laughter on those mocking lips. Another loud snap made her decide to check the ropes.

Easing herself out, an inch at a time, she sneaked carefully round the pegs, glad of the moonlight. Relieved that all the threads were taut, she stood up and glanced at the camp. In one of the caravans a light burnt and she wished she had a similar aid, so she could read. A good book would drive out the tormenting thoughts of the man who had so deeply disturbed her. She went to the car and took out her jacket. She pulled her sneakers on and set off, stepping lightly over the grass and then on to the sand. Without thinking she made for the Rangitira and paused to admire it, as it stood looking more lordly than ever.

'Young maidens should beware or they might succumb to the man of the sea.'

The deep voice made her gasp and she spun round to see the vague shape of a man seated against the log. A fishing line explained his presence.

'Trudi, isn't it?'

'How did you know?' Surprise overcame her natural courtesy.

'The man of the sea told me, of course. A beautiful woman will walk the sands at midnight.' He chuckled as he declaimed, then added conversationally, 'He had the time wrong, of course, but only by a couple of hours.'

Trudi wished she could see a little more clearly. The voice sounded teasingly familiar. The man swung the rod and the easy grace as he moved silhouetted him blackly against the sands. Before she could see his face he moved again and with a quicksilver movement tossed his coat on to the log and gestured to her to sit.

'Sir Walter Raleigh?' she questioned lightly.

'I'm my own man.'

It was strangely companionable sitting staring out at the vast seas. The line moved slightly but the hands merely settled it.

'Have you caught anything?' she asked.

'More than you dream,' he answered cryptically.

Again the laughter in the voice was oddly disarming, but she moved farther back, aware that the light fell on her face, yet shadowed his.

'Couldn't you sleep?'

The voice was gentle and she responded immediately, guessing he was Maria's fisherman.

'No! Maria fell asleep straight away, but I started thinking the tent might collapse.' She chuckled a little wryly. 'I hadn't realised that tents are so noisy. Ours goes snap more often than a popgun, and the sea saying its litany didn't help.'

This time the laughter was open and the richness of the voice warmed. 'I'm sorry it's not as you expected.'

'Don't misunderstand me. It's my inexperience, not Bell Bay's fault. It's beautiful. Look how the moonlight turns the wave crests to silver. It even makes the foam on the sand look like silver tatting on a collar.' Trudi stopped herself, realising how odd her words sounded. 'Sorry, I don't often go into rhapsodies!'

'Don't apologise, you're right—it is beautiful.' He moved closer and turned to take her hand in an oddly intimate gesture. At that moment the fishing line began to sing and he moved forward to adjust it. The moonlight fell on him revealing the powerful physique and the angles of his face.

'You!'

The word broke from Trudi with the shock. She felt herself become rigid, knowing that he was smiling faintly at her surprise. Clearly he had the upper hand, and she writhed inwardly at letting the hunk see her feelings.

The softness of her gown slipped into her fingers and she wondered what arrogant thoughts he had when she had approached him in her nightwear. She pulled her jacket closer, her thoughts tumbling in a kaleidoscope.

'Oh, come now, don't pretend.' He spoke smoothly, winding the line up.

'Why, you presumptuous . . .' Words temporarily failed her in her rage. 'Just who do you think you are?'

'Dan Johnson.' He spoke softly yet there was a dangerous silence that followed as though the mere mention of his name would quieten her.

'So what!' Trudi flared. 'You know I didn't mean that. As though I'd look at you!'

'A cat may look at a king,' Dan Johnson quoted.

'Well, I'm not a cat and I'm not looking,' Trudi snapped. 'I'm not interested in men. I'm a career girl. Thank goodness it's not necessary for a woman to have a husband to be fulfilled today.'

'In your case that attitude is probably right. Why inflict such a proud, stubborn nature on a poor, lonely male?'

'Hmph!' Trudi snorted inelegantly.

'Now how am I to interpret that? The lady agrees, so she's wiser than I thought; occasionally speechless, so she's learnt the value of silence! Remarkable.'

He leaned closer and Trudi felt her temper explode again.

'Typical, arrogant male; making snap judgments without basing your decision on anything more substantial than a minute's conversation!'

His full-throated roar of laughter would have scared any fish within sound. Realising the trap she had dug for herself, Trudi joined in the laughter.

'At least you've got a sense of humour. Tell me why you decided to be a career woman.'

Trudi stared out over the moonlit sea. The question made her examine herself. Why had she decided to be a career woman? she asked herself silently. For a second she had a momentary vision of the meeting at the pool. Was it so that she could be safe from the temptation offered by the gleaming eyes of a man such as Dan Johnson?

CHAPTER TWO

TRUDI became aware of the man waiting quietly beside her. His stillness seemed a part of the night.

'I don't think I ever consciously made the decision, it just happened,' she was forced to concede. 'I'd wanted to be a barrister, but by the time I reached university level it wasn't possible, so I joined Maugh's Fashions as a machinist.'

She looked out to sea, feeling the agony that decision had caused her.

'And your sister?'

'Maria's a barrister.' She did not even try to keep the pride from her voice.

'You gave your sister your dream.'

His perception startled her. She had to be honest.

'Not entirely. Maria had always wanted to become one. She had the brains, even won a scholarship. There was no stopping her.' She added dryly, 'Until John came on the scene and they married.'

'And is she happy?'

'Blissfully.' She had to admit it.

'And you? Still singing "The Song of the Shirt"?'

'In a manner of speaking. I'm Production Manager at the factory. We make clothes for women who appreciate "something a little different".'

'Like the Emperor?' His eyes glimmered in the light. 'Production Manager sounds important. I imagine you didn't walk into that job?'

'Hardly! I went to night school and did business administration and tried to do some accountancy units.

I was doing extra shifts and one day I fell asleep, and for me it was the luckiest snooze ever. The boss was very kind. He said I could start working in the different sections to learn from the inside. I guess you could say I was a Jack of all trades,' Trudi chuckled.

'Jill, at the very least. One surprising point. Are all the men in this factory blind? You're quite startlingly lovely.'

Trudi looked at the man, wishing the shape of the nearby rocks didn't shadow him. His compliment had been merely a statement of fact. Stewart had said the same thing, she remembered. Stewart had been in charge of advertising and sales. He was charming, urbane, and handsome. Nearly all the girls had been green with envy when she had been sent into Stewart's section to learn the basics of his craft. Stewart had taken one crushing look at her dyed school blouses and clean but far from new jeans and told her to wear something presentable. Sales staff, he informed her crisply, were expected to look as if they believed in their product. As he told her to go back to machining till she could appear in more suitable attire, she had been crushed, and studying the carefully worked out family budget again, she could not see how she could comply.

The same night her mother had announced her intention of marrying again. Both Trudi and Maria had been surprised. They knew their mother had been spending a lot of time during the day helping a friend with his children, as his wife had died. Engrossed in work and study, neither had been aware of the loneliness of their mother. After the announcement events had moved with speed. Almost overnight the house had been sold. Their new family lived in Rangiora and they had quickly decided that the most sensible solution was for the two girls to move into a flat. For the first time Trudi found herself with money in her pocket.

It had been a real thrill to chat with Rita, the friendly forewoman, about making several new outfits. Using the staff cost scheme, she had been more than happy with the change in her appearance.

Stewart had approved, and Trudi found herself in a world she had only read about. She was taken to expensive restaurants, and wined and dined clients under Stewart's guidance. It had been natural that she should have fallen in love with him. When he was out of town she missed him deeply. She waited desperately for him to mention marriage, but gradually she realised that their relationship was doomed. Despite Stewart's seeming openness there was a reserve on some aspects which didn't tally with her own knowledge. As she got to know the routine of his department she knew that Stewart was lying at times.

Her own intelligence told her that she had to ask him if he was married, but it had still shocked her when he had admitted it, with a laughing scorn for her naïvety and innocence.

The experience had hurt. Trudi had given her heart and she felt as though it had been crushed. The whirr of a fishing line brought her back to the present, and with a wry grin she wondered if she should now be thanking Stewart. If it hadn't been for him she would never have buried herself so much in her work.

'So there was someone. Do you still judge all by the one man?'

'No. Only the dangerous ones.' Trudi spoke without thinking.

'You don't look a coward,' he observed.

'Looks can deceive.' She spoke without bitterness, she realised, and the knowledge cheered her. 'I've a challenging job, I have a satisfying life. Just this past year, we've increased sales, built up the part-time staff, put in a new lounge and now we are looking at export orders.'

'Quite the model factory!'

'Far from it. But at least we've made a start. Even the outside looks different now. I love gardening, but there isn't room at the flat. At the factory there was a long strip of ground where things were dumped. We had it cleared and instant lawn put down and flowers planted, even a tree. It's much nicer sitting out there than in the staff room.'

'You'll be running the whole place soon,' Dan Johnson observed.

'I do frequently,' laughed Trudi. 'That's why I wanted to find a place without telephones.'

'Bell Bay should be a change. How much work did you bring?'

'I've been talking too much. As a matter of fact just plans for a new distribution method.'

They both laughed then and Trudi thought that she had never spent such a vigil before.

'Watch yourself,' he warned, 'or you might find you leave part of your heart with the Rangitira.'

She knew he had turned towards her and she stood up abruptly. For an instant she thought the man was about to kiss her and she was oddly breathless at his closeness. Swiftly she moved back, aware of the sudden dancing of her heart. However, he merely bent to the creel beside him and she guessed she had been mistaken.

'The wind has changed,' he remarked.

'You're right. I'd better get back to the tent—it's

probably stopped flapping. Goodnight.'

Inwardly pleased with her outward calm, Trudi set off down the beach.

Dan Johnson did not offer to walk with her back to the tent. Scudding clouds racing across the moon meant that the sand was flooded alternately with light and dark like an old movie. Once Trudi glanced back and she saw his silhouette again as he stood staring out to sea. He reminded her of the Rangitira, now almost fully exposed by the waves. A stray thought niggled at her as she wondered if fishermen went surf casting when the tide was on its way out. Yet he couldn't have known she would appear. She shivered suddenly despite the warmth, thinking that Dan Johnson was too attractive, too dangerously male.

The sun was well up when she woke. She saw that Maria had disappeared and she glanced out of the tent. Maria was dressed and was carrying sticks and driftwood to their fireplace. Lazily Trudi yawned, then glanced instinctively out to the beach. She frowned, wondering what was missing, then realised that the Rangitira was gone. For a moment, she marvelled, then laughed at her own stupidity. The tides would have changed and covered the rock. The dancing water much calmer than before, the sun shining on the white cliffs making them shimmer, and the birdsong from the bush all delighted her. She wished that she could spend all her holiday in this idyllic setting, then remembered that Maria had to return to her husband the next day.

At the back of her mind the thought formed that she could stay on by herself. The spot was a secluded one, the few other campers sufficiently desirous of their own privacy to appreciate her own, and she had everything

she needed. She could buy more supplies for herself at
the shops when she dropped Maria, she decided. If a
storm arose she could shelter in the car and if it
remained wet she could easily pack up and return to
the flat.

The heat in the tent was becoming unbearable and
she felt sticky. Remembering the cold showers was
enough to make her postpone them, but the aroma of
breakfast sent her helter-skelter towards the white
concrete structure. Contrary to expectations the toilet
block was clean, and Trudi even found herself appreciating the icy water as it sprayed over her body.
She dressed and made her way to the tent where Maria
was in the act of serving the breakfast.

'Tremendous! I feel hungry, fancy eating such a
huge breakfast.' The bacon, tomatoes and toast were a
far cry from her usual meal as she dived out to work,
but she enjoyed them immensely.

'You were a real sleepyhead this morning, Trudi.
Couldn't you sleep last night?' asked Maria.

'No! You didn't help, going to sleep straight away!'
Trudi chuckled. 'I sat there tossing and getting hotter,
so I went for a walk along the beach. It was beautiful.
I must have sat for hours.'

She scooped up the last piece of toast, appreciating
the wood smoked flavour it had. For some reason she
didn't want to tell Maria about the quiet vigil she had
shared with Dan Johnson. As she cleaned up the dishes
she noticed a family set off from one of the caravans
towards the beach. They waved a casual salute and she
waved back. Another family group joined the first and
set off for the small bay.

Maria and Trudi tidied their tent and washed out
their clothes, pegging them on their temporary line.
They prepared a large bottle of drink and put fruit in

their pockets, then set off for the line of bush behind the camping grounds. The stile must have been set up years before and the girls clambered over it. Surprisingly, a well defined track opened before them and they followed it, finding themselves in scrubby bush. Manuka, with its dainty white and pink starred blooms, edged the path and beside the purple leaves of the native akeake provided a natural beauty that contrasted with the green of the lacebark and lemonwood. Imperceptibly the vegetation changed and the trees grew much larger, even the manuka growing to twice the size of the earlier four-foot bushes. The floor was a riot of tangled vines and ferns, and the tiny natural watercourse, dried now by the heat of summer, provided the only other pathway. Occasionally the girls saw clumps of taller trees until they came out on to a natural grassland. Here the skyline was clear as the limestone cliffs reared ahead, decorated only with the topknot of cabbage trees.

On one side the bush spread back towards more hills, but the open grassland leading up to the top of the cliffs held definite appeal for Trudi.

'Hey, let's stop here and eat, Trudi. Up there it will be like an oven.'

'I guess you're right.' Reluctantly she sat under a tree and handed the heavy bottle to Maria, then munched noisily on an apple.

'Mm, these first-of-the-season apples are lovely.' She smiled at Maria. 'Isn't that view magnificent, you can see for miles.'

'I must tell John. Even if we came up for the day.'

The little bay below them was partially hidden but she could see their tent and one of the caravans. It revealed a sweep of the coastline and through a gap in the hills Trudi saw a shining expanse of roof. She knew it would be one of the workers' bungalows for the Ti Kouka estate and wondered briefly what it would mean to live in such an isolated place. She had loved the look of the homestead and the beauty that surrounded it. Even as she looked she saw a man on horseback, riding along the hill to the side of the house, and she spent some time wondering what glinted as he moved. Maria finally guessed it was binoculars, and Trudi felt indignant that they should be spied upon until she recollected that the use of the binoculars could save many a long mile of riding.

'You know, I think it's that nice man we met at the stream; the hunk!' Maria exclaimed, and waved gladly.

Trudi pulled her sister's arm down and then was furious with herself. Dan Johnson would undoubtedly have seen them and had probably already identified them. She poked out her tongue saucily, to let him know she was not one of the mindless ones, then was horrified at her own childishness. Thinking guiltily that he couldn't possibly have seen at the distance, she scrambled back into the bush, instinctively hiding from the figure.

'Let's go back. As you said, it's far too hot to climb further and the water should be cool.'

Ignoring the beautiful scenery, the dainty ferns and the flowering bushes, Trudi fled down the bush track. Maria raced after her and both were breathless when they finally reached the stile, and Trudi leant on it, gasping.

'You look about sixteen,' laughed Maria. 'If the staff could see you now!'

Trudi knew her sister was right. She felt ridiculously carefree and lighthearted.

The perfection of the spot with the wise old Rangitira held her in its grip. They splashed about in the sheltered curve of the beach. It was fun, and afterwards while Maria lay soaking up the sun, Trudi went back to the campsite and began preparing dinner. The steak had thawed and would barbecue well, and she peeled a few potatoes and opened a packet of dried mixed vegetables. The heat of the day had made the peaches she had bought look decidedly messy, so she salvaged the best and stewed them, then burnt the rubbish. She was surprised how late it was; at home she could guess the time with a reasonable accuracy, but here all the guidelines were different.

Looking up at the trees they had reached that morning, she saw the horseman had reached the site where they had stopped for lunch. She watched idly as he swung off the horse and then stooped to pick up something that glinted in the sun. In sudden humiliation Trudi realised it must have been the bottle she had carted up there for drinks. Her cheeks flamed as she knew the damage such a bottle could do if it broke. Miserably she crawled into the tent to hide, imagining the lashing scorn of the man at the creek. Instinctively she knew it was Dan Johnson.

The smoke of the campfire reminded her that she could not abandon their meat, so she crept out again. To her relief the horseman was gone, and she was just wondering about calling Maria when she returned. The flavour of the food they agreed was delicious and afterwards they made a bigger pile of driftwood ready for the next morning's campfire. Maria went off to talk to one of the families and Trudi lay back enjoying the peace.

A four-wheeled-drive vehicle roared noisily into the camp, completely shattering the silence. To her disgust the vehicle made unerringly for their campfire and pulled up beside their car. The bronzed muscular figure who stepped from it was familiar.

'Good evening. I'm returning the bottle you left by the trees at the top of the ridge.'

His eyes seemed to hold the frost of Antarctica in them. Trudi took the half full bottle and apologised. She would have found it missing at washing up time and retrieved it the next morning, she explained weakly.

'I understood you were leaving tomorrow?'

'We were, but I'd like to ask the owners about staying on. Could you tell me if we should ask at the homestead?'

'How long do you intend to stay?'

'I've no idea. It really depends on the weather—if it stays like this it might be for a fortnight, if it rains, earlier.'

'Afraid you'll melt?'

'Definitely not. I have no intention of putting myself in a state of being uncomfortable.'

To her surprise he smiled. 'I'll pass it on. There'll be no need for you to make a special trip.'

Trudi was sincerely glad to see Maria trotting up with her arms full of firewood.

'So you're the worker in the family!' observed Dan Johnson.

'Hardly! My sister leaves me for dead!' Maria's gay laugh rang out as she corrected him. 'How super of you to visit us. Would you like a cup of tea? With the fire on it won't take long. My husband says there's nothing quite like billy tea, and I think he's right.'

'No, thank you, I just stopped for a moment.' He turned and looked searchingly at Trudi. 'Sleep well.'

With a casual wave he was in the truck and reversing it expertly. It made Trudi feel rather better when she saw him emptying and burning the refuse from the drums around the camp, and the horridness of the job made her even feel a little sorry for him. Idly she supposed he was used to such messy work and it was probably he who kept the showers and toilets clean. Trudi stowed the bottle with her name neatly plastered on the base into the car. Whereas before she had felt supremely contented, now she was as restless as she had been the evening before.

'Let's go for a walk along the beach, Maria,' she suggested.

'I've just come back, remember!'

Trudi sat down again. She didn't want to walk along the beach on her own while that hunk, as Maria had called him, was in the camp. Her feelings annoyed her. Dan Johnson was obviously the most junior employee at the farm, yet he rode around looking as if he was the king of the earth. The strange antagonism that flared so easily between them had been evident in the reproof over the bottle.

She recalled that he had neither begged her to stay nor pleaded with her to remain, yet his taunting over the possibility of her melting had been calculated. He had even appreciated the coolness of her reply. Even his knowing glance and that apparently innocent 'Sleep well' had held the sense of a challenge. Trudi thrust another log on to the fire and stared at the flames firing blue-green for a moment, then turning to orange and red.

'Maria, I think I'll stay at Bell Bay tomorrow,' she decided.

'Trudi, you can't!'

'Why not? It's a beautiful place, it's isolated, yet there are respectable families around. I'd be a great deal safer here than at any hotel in town.'

'But on your own, Trudi.'

'Listen, Maria, I'm a perfectly capable person. The tent is no problem, we've already proved that,' she carried on, seeing her sister's stormy face. 'I can cope with the fire, and the food situation I can rectify at that general store not far from the junction. The bus from Picton will pass through about four, I'd guess. You'll still be in Christchurch in time.'

'So long as I can meet John's plane. I wonder how he's getting on. I miss him.'

Seeing the expression on her sister's face, Trudi turned away. Briefly she wondered if she would ever love a man the way her sister loved her John, then dismissed the thought as ridiculous. As she had told Dan Johnson, she was a career girl, she had no intention of being a slave for any man. Dan Johnson might have a magnetism she found attractive, but there the matter ended. She would keep right away from him in the time at Bell Bay.

The first step was to stop thinking about him, but later as she lay in her sleeping bag she found his penetrating eyes and bronzed body invading her rest. She wriggled in the folds, reminding herself that even paradise had a serpent.

In the morning they went for an early swim at the little bay and then made breakfast.

'Pity John can't join you here,' remarked Trudi, 'we're becoming quite proficient with our fire.'

'I wish he could. Perhaps next year for our holidays John and I could come here. He'd love the bush and the beach. He's not going to believe how good we are with our cooking. I can never get the tomatoes to taste like this at home. Wood smoke has a definite flavour.'

'Shall we go into the bush again or laze on the beach?'

'Just laze is my vote. I want to improve my tan.'

Maria looked smugly at her golden limbs.

'I think I might have a look for driftwood shapes while you snooze. I noticed some really odd ones earlier.'

'Well, if you see that gorgeous man ask him about the bus times,' said Maria somnolently. 'Ah, this is the life!'

Privately Trudi hoped she wouldn't see the tall figure of Dan Johnson. The man had invaded her dreams and she had no desire to see him when awake. Deliberately she walked to the small cove where some of the other campers welcomed her. They conversed, idly exchanging details, and finding one lady was a mine of local information, Trudi obtained the afternoon bus times. As she sauntered down to the Bell Bay site she picked up small white pebbles and odd tiny pieces of wood for decoration.

'Treasure-hunting?' asked Maria. 'While you were away some bellbirds started singing in the bush. It sounded beautiful, just like tinkling chimes. I suppose I'd better pack my gear.'

'I've found the bus times for you. It fits in well with meeting John.'

As Trudi waved her sister off in the large coach to Christchurch she replaced her sunhat on a jaunty angle and went into the corner store. The shopkeeper was evidently accustomed to supplying odd bits and pieces and Trudi had roughed out a list earlier. With arms fully laden she was glad of the shopkeeper's assistance with some of the goods. She certainly wouldn't starve, she thought, as she drove back to the now familiar track. As she went past Ti Kouka she slowed automatically, but there was no sign of the junior employee who had so disturbed her. She could hardly blame Ti Kouka for the hard muscles and arrogance of Dan

Johnson and her own reaction to him.

Deliberately she looked away and concentrated on her driving. Slowing to ford the stream that meandered across the road, she guessed that in winter time it would carry more than a torrent across the beach to the sea. Probably one would have to have a four-wheel-drive vehicle to negotiate it then. Trudi winced as one of the large boulders rocked against and scraped the bottom of her precious car. Obviously the county grader had long since given up the struggle to keep up with this stretch of the road.

The quiet of the evening camp was broken only by the distant call of a couple of children, and she could see an older couple cooking a meal over a barbecue by their tent.

It seemed strange without Maria and she decided to go for a walk along by the sea. She slipped into her sandals as the sand could still burn at that hour and went to see the Rangitira, but even he was 'not at home'. The shore held lots of other enchantments, and Trudi walked along, picking up more of the tiny smooth white almost flat pebbles and pocketing them. She saw a piece of driftwood and admired its tuatara-like shape. With very little whittling of the mouth and the knots forming the bulbous eyes it would look very dragonlike. She decided to try carving it later.

Two people were fishing on the rocks by the cliffs and they told her it would be possible at low tide to get right round. She determined to do that the very next day, then smiled, as she didn't even have an idea of when the tides changed. These expert fishermen could no doubt tell her exactly.

The jeep was at the campsite and she watched casually as Dan Johnson lifted a drum of rubbish into the back. She grinned, hoping he was finding it a hateful job, then wondered at her own maliciousness. The man was occupying far too much of her thoughts. She went into the tent and lay down lazily on the foam pad. It was stupid to think about such a man, she told herself.

She grabbed one of the books, then discovered that although it might be light enough for wandering around, it certainly wasn't light enough to read. She put the book back in the car, having already discovered how damp things could get in even a dry tent. She pulled out her sleep attire and a dressing gown and put them into the tent.

Gratefully Trudi remembered the driftwood. Carving its prehistoric shape would keep her mind occupied. Somewhere in her cutlery she had a small sharp knife, and she rattled around in the container, discovering it by nearly cutting herself. Perched in the middle of the plank seat, she sang quietly to herself as she studied the wood. Her first cut was more a scrape and she was surprised at the hardness of the wood. She dug in harder and achieved a more satisfactory result.

Unaware of the passage of time, she was engrossed in the work and only the fading of the firelight made her desist. Trudi walked over to the shower and toilet block, stumbling a little in the dark, wishing she had remembered to carry her torch. The shower was too icy to stand under for long, so she was soon marching down the hill again. She carried her day clothes in a small linen bag as she decided it was a great deal easier to change into her nightwear in the shower recess than in the confines of a low tent. The coolness of the silk felt soft against her skin. Trudi admitted that her nightwear and lingerie were her pet extravagances; she loved the soft feminine dainty garments. The outfit she wore tonight was the colour of the sea at twilight. On impulse she wondered if the Rangitira was on view and she detoured to the beach to see him.

The slap and wash of the waves told her the tide was receding, and she ran, dumping her gear at the edge of the sand. The eyes and nose appeared and disappeared in the waves. There was a magic in the night which was intoxicating and Trudi found herself, after a brief glance at the silent camp to make sure everyone was asleep, throwing off her dressing gown, aware of the freedom of the beach. Exultantly, she laughed and danced, feeling the night air lift her hair. The sand skipped as she ran along it, dancing and frolicking in wide, ever-increasing circles until she collapsed weakly in a heap by the sand in front of the old Rangitira. Totally lightheaded, she scrambled to her feet, calling out to the song of the waves.

'Hey, Rangitira, you're my man. I dare you to come and play!' She was up and dancing, again spinning to some secret melody.

Still laughing at herself, she stopped aghast as a dark shape began to move towards her, swimming powerfully through the water. Mesmerised, she stood poised as the shape revealed itself to be some godlike figure, water pouring off the bulging muscles of the black-smith-like chest and the slim hips. For a moment the moonlight showed the black alien figure moving towards her, then a cloud shadowed the light. Terrified, Trudi began to run along the beach., her heartbeats making so much noise she could only just hear the thud of her pursuer's feet. Too late she realised that in her fright she had taken off around the small cove and away from the camp. Her breath was coming in short painful bursts and she was just about to run out of beach when she remembered the track by the cliffs.

With the tide on its way out she still had a chance to escape. The wind seemed to be crying to her to stop, but she ran on.

The white cliffs glinted silver in front of her, cutting off her progress. Glancing behind her, she could not see the creature, but she dared not stop to check. Gasping, she turned towards the sea, hoping to find the path round the rocks. She called out, hoping Dan Johnson or the fishermen would hear her. If only she had listened to Maria! she thought despairingly. Could she find the path before the creature seized her?

CHAPTER THREE

TRUDI'S feet flew on the wet sand. The wind seemed to be crying to her to stop, but she barely slowed as she approached the cliffs. Only as she reached the rocks did she see the creature an instant before she cannoned into it. Her scream was silenced as giant black cold clammy arms closed around her. Her struggles were futile as the iron strength held her easily, and in desperation she bit at the horrid rubbery skin. It was a relief to hear the imprecation that followed, telling her that the creature that held her was no sea monster but a mere man in a wet-suit. She kicked out, glad of his automatic release, only to be pulled with him as they both fell.

'And to think I thought you were a nereid inviting me to some delightful fantasy!' he muttered, when at last she lay stilled by his strength. 'You're more like some bride of Dracula!'

'Thanks very much! You frightened the seven bells out of me, suddenly appearing out of the water like that!' Trudi's breath was still short, but at least she was no longer in a state of terror, having recognised the man.

He had the temerity to begin chuckling, as he hauled off the rubber suit.

'Maybe you should learn not to play dares. You need a lesson, young woman.'

'Well, I certainly don't intend taking lessons from you, you ... you ...' she spluttered as she searched for the right devastating phrase, 'you overgrown hunk of masculinity!'

43

'Lesson one, young nereid, I don't like rude names.' He waited for an apology and when there was only a proud lift of her head his hand pulled her towards him with that same inexorable strength and she felt her mouth taken and crushed. She was aware that he was punishing her for the taunt, and she struggled, trying to move away from the hard fire of his mouth. She felt her whole body tighten against his, and softened, wanting his caress in the mad moonlight, then she realised how crazily she was behaving.

'I'm sorry,' she whispered huskily.

Immediately Dan released her. She sat up, still shaking, and he stood up and pulled her to her feet.

'I'm sorry too, nereid. I didn't mean to startle you and when you took off towards the cove I was afraid you'd try something dangerous, like attempting the cliff track.'

Trudi glanced past him in horror at the waves crashing over the rocks at the base of the cliffs. In her terror she hadn't had time to realise how impossible it would have been.

'It's not to be attempted in moonlight by a stranger, even a nereid. I'll take you round to Seal Bay tomorrow if you like, to make up for giving you a fright. Meet me here at two-thirty and I'll see you get round and back safely.'

'You'd better not, your boss might throw a spanner. Don't junior employees have to work pretty hard on places like Ti-Kouka?'

'Not as hard as the boss!' He grinned suddenly. 'I can take a little time off, occasionally. We're not without some of the more civilised attributes of the city. I'll even offer to escort you back to your residence, just to make sure Rangitira doesn't frighten you again.'

'I'm perfectly all right now. I think Rangitira would offer me considerably less trouble.' Trudi saw the moonlight catch the gleam in his eyes for a moment and she hastily added a few conciliatory words.

'Thank you, but I shall be fine. Besides, there's all your gear.'

She turned and walked down the beach. The sand felt cold under her feet and she was suddenly aware of her gossamer night attire clinging to her. She would have liked to run from the tall dark shadow standing there, but she refused to show how upset she had been.

Only when she had turned the corner did she run as fast as she could to her gown, pull into its comforting warmth and collect her bag. In less than a minute she had made her tent, but as she had sand in her clothes she was forced to open the car door to get some more. Shivering, she changed, hating the fact that there was not room to stand in the confines of the tent. She would have loved to have made herself a hot drink, but her fire was dead, not even a spark remaining. Snuggling into her sleeping bag, she pulled a rug over the top, grateful for the warmth. Even so it was a long time before she stopped shivering, but in her heart she knew it was not only caused by the cold. It had been so long since a man had kissed her and the sensation had touched something she had thought was as dead as the ashes of the camp fire.

Trudi moaned softly, as she realised that her carefully guarded barricade had been demolished so easily. She had been forced into that first kiss, but her flesh shivered again as the memory of those moments on the sand could not be forgotten. She had enjoyed the feel of the hard flesh, the firm muscles which had imprisoned her, and to her intense humiliation the arrogant Dan Johnson had known it. Tentatively she felt her lips. She had known the man was dangerous, the minute she had set eyes on him at the creek. The cold treatment she had given him there was the only way to react.

If he came close again she would be in deep water, and she had worked for too long remembering that men could not be trusted. He was definitely the most dangerous man she had ever encountered. Physically their bodies reacted, she told herself, adding that it would be the last time she would allow such a challenge. She had fired him by her struggles and he wasn't the type to allow an insult to pass unnoticed.

The next day she would not allow him to so much as offer a helping hand. She would use the same defences she had used so expertly against many of the men with whom she came into contact through work. She would be cool, logical and dignified, and soon her immunity would recover. It had been the fault of the moonlight and the delicious abandonment she had felt dancing on the silvered beach.

She felt a hot tear burn down her cheek and was surprised by the emotions that were see-sawing through her. In part it was outrage, in part anger, in part desolation, and it was a relief to feel the tears spurt. Trudi brushed them away and sniffed. The whole incident had become out of proportion, she told herself. After all, what was a kiss? She had been kissed before. It was just the effect of the night, plus the strange chemistry they had been instantly aware of when their eyes had met back at the creek.

With a sigh she realised she should not go with the man to see the hidden bay the next day. With typical male arrogance he had presumed she would fall at his feet at the idea, but now she realised that she had side-stepped the issue. A smile touched her lips; she was not going to be any man's plaything, she would follow her own terms.

The sound of the waves seemed to have made a song as she woke the next morning. Again the tent was stifling hot and she had no idea of the time. For once she was uncaring, she was living to nature's clock. She sang softly as she performed sketchy ablutions and washed out her clothes. Only as she pegged out the soft shimmering green silk nightgown did the frown return and her song faded away. After breakfast Trudi decided that it would be a good time to explore the beach in the opposite direction. The tent took only a few minutes to tidy, then she made some lunch and took a book, a rug, a drink and her work notes in a pack and set off along the beach. Once away from the shelter of the point the sea crashed and dashed itself along the huge rocks. Many were like giant stepping-stones and she moved past them slowly, admiring their stark beauty. She could see the road she had followed, then saw the homestead in the distance. She picked up her pack and moved on hurriedly, wanting to get out of sight of the large glinting windows and any possible glimpse of the man who had upset her.

Briefly she wondered if she was being fair to Dan. He had probably had to get time off and he was not the type to like asking for favours. It was very bad manners to leave no word for him, and she tried to remember any time she had done anything similar in the past. She knew she had never been so discourteous, but then savagely she was glad that such an arrogant creature would cool his heels. He would realise that she was not interested in him and he would leave her alone. The battle would be over. Trudi sighed as she gazed at the sea, wondering why she felt so defeated. She supposed it was just her upbringing, feeling guilt over failing to leave a message.

A large group of rocks formed a distinctive pattern on the sand, almost like an island, and she headed towards them, deciding she could rest there and read or gaze at the sea. She dumped her bag and began climbing. The rocks were quite easy to climb and on top she found a hollow which was sheltered by a higher rock behind. Chuckling to herself with joy, she clambered down and hauled up her pack. Although the rug had been heavy to carry she was glad of her foresight now as she rolled one half to form a backrest and the other to sit on. She gazed at the sea, then picked up the pencil and paper with the intention of working out some of the details of the latest distribution plans, but found herself sketching the shape of the rocks around her.

Amused and promising herself that no one would ever see her sketches, she began to shade in the line of the rock, then she noticed that she was drawing the Rangitira, but he looked alarmingly like Dan Johnson. She scored through it and ripped the paper to shreds, firing it around her. The sea wind, instead of taking it out to sea, flung it back to her, so she stuffed it in her pack. The wretched man seemed to have irritated her, and she put away the pencil and began eating her lunch. Idly she wondered about the time. Her perch was safe; the rock where she sat was too dry ever to have been covered by high tide. Lower, the rocks were slippery and festooned with weed, showing the high water mark. Trudi felt slightly sleepy and using her pack as a pillow she curled up, feeling oddly lulled by the distant murmur of the sea. She realised that she had had very little sleep the night before owing to the emotions she had experienced, and she felt oddly pleased at the image of the big man waiting for her at the camp.

'Serve you right,' she muttered as she closed her eyes.

Her dreams were mixed with the sound of the sea and nightmare pictures of the giant chasing her and then turning into a seagull hopelessly calling her name. The sound woke her and she rubbed the sleep from her eyes, then moved her aching limbs.

The full implication of her situation took but a moment to seep through. She had been totally stupid to have slept in such a situation. The shore was not a long distance away, but the size of the crashing waves which had turned her rocks into an island alarmed her. A seagull flew overhead, his noisy cry laughing at her position. Trudi glanced at her watch, then remembered that she had deliberately left it off. She looked around her, trying to estimate the depth of the tide; too late she remembered the dampness of the sand she had been walking along to avoid the heat and the sea at the edge of her rocks. That alone should have told her that she was in an area normally surrounded at high tide.

'Trudi, you're silly, but you're in no danger,' she told herself. 'Just sit tight, until the tide changes again, then you can climb down again and return to camp. Just a bit lucky that you've still got those two apples and a sandwich left and even a couple of mouthfuls of drink.'

She stood up and walked carefully around her perch, then clambered down and peered over the edge. All she received was a splash of cold water, so she backed away cautiously and climbed up to her rug again. She wondered if the sea was at the peak or if it was still coming in.

She looked at the sky, wishing she had some idea whether it was five, six or seven o'clock. Vaguely she remembered Dan saying it was low tide at two-thirty. She had a mouthful of drink, wondering just at what time the tide would retreat and leave her able to clamber down. A schoolgirl memory of tides being twelve hours from low tide to low tide teased at her and she thought grimly of herself trying to make her way down the rocks in the moonlight at two-thirty in the early morning. She told herself she must be wrong, but just to be on the safe side she recapped her drink bottle firmly. If the waves eased she could swim the few yards to the shore, but to attempt it at the moment would be folly.

'Cheer up, Trudi,' she scolded herself. 'You can do that distribution change costing without the telephone or the thousand and one things that usually interrupt you. You always said you needed a desert island for a bit of peace and quiet, and now you've got one. Besides, it's sensible to keep busy,' she admonished herself.

She picked up the sandwich and ate half and one of the apples, tucking the other back, just in case she was hungry later. She ate it slowly, wishing the sea air did not make her feel so conscious of her appetite. Deliberately she looked around in case anyone was in sight, then sank back into the shelter again. She would do it several times, she told herself, just in case anyone was looking for her. She reminded herself that no one would even notice if she was gone. Dan would have realised she didn't intend to keep the date and he would have returned home. The other campers would all be busy with their own interests.

For once Trudi felt it difficult to immerse herself in

the intricacies of the plans. Without access to her calculator she had to do every sum mentally and it took longer than she had thought to plan and cost. She kept herself busy working out the details and when she had finally exhausted all the possibilities her brain could give her, she wrote them all out again in order of preference before putting the book away carefully in her pack.

Again she stood up and did a little walk round her rocks, then gathered more of the dry sticks and seaweed as a cushion. She snuggled into her rug, aware of the change in temperature, as the sun lowered itself slowly and gently into the sea. For an instant the whole rim of the sky was lit, turning the sea and the tips of the hills behind her to gold, then it seemed to grow dark.

'Trudi, this is where you've got to be patient!' she lectured herself. One of the giant black-backed gulls came to join her on the rocks. Although she knew it was stupid she felt almost honoured by its presence. She ate her half sandwich, then seeing the bird's eye on her she broke off a piece and threw it at him. He eyed her for a moment, then swept on the bread and flew off with it in his beak.

'You daft creature, Trudi,' she told herself. 'That bird can supply himself any time, whereas you're feeling hungry already. And you're wide awake, not the slightest bit sleepy, having slept for hours. It's just as well you have your jeans on or you'd have had a bad dose of sunburn, if not sunstroke!'

The crashing of the waves seemed impossibly loud and she imagined the spray coming closer.

The hills and the sea turned black and the first pale star appeared. Much later she could pick up the three bright jewels on Orion's Belt and she could trace his shape, then she could make out the Seven Sisters just

ahead of him. She was going to set a similar gulf between Dan Johnson and herself. In fact, she thought
tiredly, she had already done so. He wouldn't come
looking for her, he'd prefer more compliant game.

'Bother the wretched man, he won't even let me
alone for a few moments,' she muttered angrily to herself. 'If I ever get married I'd want to marry someone
like dear old Mr Maugh. He'd be kind and considerate
and I'd be able to do anything I wanted at the factory.
He's been a wonderful employer and he'd never let me
down.'

Trudi thought it all over carefully. Love was a
luxury she did not want. Love was ephemeral, changing like the patterns of the wind, she told herself, de-
nying the small voice that whispered that true love
overcame problems and grew because of them. The
same voice told her she wasn't serious in considering
marriage for security.

She stood up slowly and glanced around. Her eyes
were quite accustomed to the night and she looked
anxiously at the waves, noting that they seemed to be
still increasing. She wished she had marked pieces of
rock earlier, so that she would know whether the tide
was going in or out. Briefly she considered doing so in
the limited light, then decided that it would be tempt-
ing fate. She glanced along the darkness of the sea, the
foam lit by the moon as it smashed on to another group
of rocks. The shore was only a pale band and she could
see nothing there against the darkness of the hills. If
Mr Maugh were in the same situation, she wondered,
what would he do? and realised he would have the great
presence of mind to sit still and be patient.

Tangling on that thought came the image of Dan
Johnson. In a similar situation she wondered what he
would do. She had to admit the man would never let

such a chance arise. For one thing he knew the sea and would have known the danger of the position. If he had sheltered there he would have made sure he left in plenty of time. The memory of his powerful arms slicing through the waves teased her, and she looked at the distance between herself and the water and realised that he would have known too if there was danger or not in the swirling waters. Almost idly she wondered if he was swimming down at the small beach of the camping ground. She considered the possibility briefly, then forced it aside. She was not interested in him at all, she reminded herself.

Her throat seemed oddly large and she uncapped the bottle and had another mouthful, being careful to save a little more. She was glad of the rug now, its woollen fibre was warm. On the rock she had at last felt the coolness of the sea and the damp and cold seemed to have penetrated her bones.

There was an eeriness that gnawed at her. The dried seaweed that she had gathered from the rock to lie on earlier protected her from the worst of the coldness of the rock, but nothing could block off her imagination. Trudi thought of Dan Johnson again, frightening her with his appearance in the wet-suit. Probably he had been crayfishing. She had a flashing vision of dozens of the crayfish scrambling up the rocks, their pincers enormous and waving. She pushed her fists into tight balls, biting back her instinct to scream. The cloud covering the moon moved away and she felt an overwhelming relief that she could see the rocks in front of her, bare and black.

Schooling herself to look in the darkened shadows for movement, she tried to cheer herself to more pleasant thoughts of her mother and her new husband and their home in the small dormitory suburb of

Christchurch. Thinking it all over she saw that her mother was happy, and Trudi knew that part of her own resentment had been anger at her father's place being usurped. With a faint wry smile she conceded that until the fisherman's question the other night she had never faced up to it.

A cloud blocked the light and she shivered, wishing it were not so dark. If only Maria were here they could tell each other stories. Maria would be able to make up a grisly anecdote about the piece of driftwood that looked like a skeletal arm and fingers. Trudi shuddered and picked it up, heaving it as far as she could, but the splash was hidden in the crash of the waves.

To cheer herself up she began singing. At first she sang pop songs and ballads and when her repertoire ran out she began on nursery rhymes.

'Trudi! Nereid!'

Instinctively she answered, then stood up in surprise. A black dripping figure appeared round the rocks, but this time she was glad to recognise Dan Johnson. She watched as he removed his flippers and hauled himself up. His wet-suit glinted over the contours of his body and the blackness seemed to be echoed by the dark spark in his eyes.

'I never heard of a nereid singing "Baa, baa, black sheep" before,' he said softly. 'All the same, I think you're more dangerous than those ancient damsels.'

'I was perfectly all right.'

'Of course! You just happened to land up on one of the most difficult pieces on the whole coastline to do your Circe act. At least you had the sense to stay put,' he added grudgingly. 'You might appreciate these.' He removed a rope and two bags tied around his back.

Two thermos flasks and some plastic-wrapped articles were in the bags. The first revealed a warm thick-knit sweater which she pulled on happily.

Eagerly she opened a flask and the tang of hot thick soup rose above the smell of the sea. She hardly noticed him stripping off some of his unwieldy gear and pulling on a thick fisherman's type of jersey which had also been wrapped in waterproof.

She drank some of the soup slowly, letting the warmth seep deliciously through her being. When Dan sat down beside her she poured him some and he smiled whimsically as though he wasn't sure whether she gave it gladly or not. Trudi felt slightly ridiculous as he glanced at her and she was sure he was remembering the drink at the creek, when she had made her antagonism so obvious.

'It was good of you to bring the hot soup,' she said. 'I was feeling hungry. Without a watch the time seemed to hang heavily and I wasn't sure just how long I'd have to wait.'

'Then you came out here at low tide? If you'd met me this afternoon it wouldn't have happened.' Dan looked at her steadily. 'If I'd known you had a rug and some drink and food I'd have let you stay.'

'Well, I didn't invite you to come and do the big hero act,' she flared. 'Nor did I say that I'd go with you to the little bay. Just who do you think you are?'

To her surprise he chuckled.

'Shakespeare must have met an ancestor of yours, I reckon. Obviously you're not injured?'

'Obviously!' Trudi snapped back.

'Well, why didn't you get off earlier?' he demanded.

Trudi hung her head. 'I fell asleep.'

He roared with laughter, but it was a jovial sound, not the nasty one she had envisaged. She was even able to grin back at him.

'We've got something in common, nereid,' he commented. 'Sure you're all right? No bumps, cuts, bruises?'

'Not one,' confessed Trudi.

To her surprise he pulled out a torch and she saw him flash it at the shore in a quick signal. The light was returned and she saw rather than heard the jeep headlights speeding away.

'Just letting the others know you were perfectly O.K. and that we can get off later,' explained Dan.

'I was planning to leave at two o'clock, if not before. It will be dry then.'

'True, but it could be dark and there's no point in getting smashed up falling from up here. A slip would mean a broken leg or worse.'

Trudi gazed at him in horror. It was bad enough to be so pleased to see him, but it was worse to be trapped with Dan Johnson in such a small area with the prospect of it lasting until two the following afternoon. She looked down at the rug she had been wrapping round her trying to keep warm, and Dan positively grinned as he sat beside her.

'O.K., lie next to me and you'll keep warm and tell me the story of your life. Unless you'd rather amuse yourself with other activities?'

There was no mistaking his meaning.

'You louse! You . . . you. . . .'

'Careful, I don't like insults, remember?' he warned.

'Well, I've no desire to spend my time chatting as though I was on a summer picnic with you!'

'Good, then let's have some fun.' He reached for her and pulled her closer, holding her firmly, as she protested.

'Relax, Trudi, I was only teasing! Tell me about Maria and her husband.'

Gradually Trudi began to unwind. She had to admit

it was rather pleasant, and certainly a lot warmer, snuggled up close to him, after the chill of the night. Besides, she reasoned, she was a lot safer talking about Maria than she would be fighting him. Oddly enough he was a good listener and there was a strange peace between them as they talked. There was something very soothing in lying next to his firm muscular body, feeling his care for her. It was just as well she had stood him up or he might begin to imagine she enjoyed it, as on that earlier occasion. In the dark it seemed easy to talk.

'So, where do you go from here? Back to the factory?'

'Yes, of course.'

'What about marriage?' he asked. 'What's this boss of yours like?'

'He's a charming man, he's been very kind to me. As a matter of fact I decided he might be a good man to marry,' Trudi said coolly. Even as she said it she knew she could never marry Mr Maugh, even if he showered her with diamonds. Yet for some strange reason she knew the thought would not please Dan Johnson.

'Why?'

She was aware of the gentle movement of his finger sketching a whirl on the point of her throat close to her ear. She tried to ignore it, but the movement was very persistent.

'Why?' he asked again.

She moved away, sitting up quickly, unable to bear the feelings that the tiny movement had caused.

'I think he's kind, he'll give me what I want, and I won't ever have to worry about money again in my life.'

'The third reason,' he muttered softly, and she felt

suddenly bereft as he stood up and flung the rug back at her. She knew he was furiously angry and she felt immediately sorry, stretching her hand to his.

'I'm sorry if that seems a lousy reason for you. I'd forgotten farm workers don't get much pay.'

'There are compensations,' he spoke shortly. 'I suppose this man is some oily suave creep who's filthy rich and that's all you care about. You wouldn't be marrying him, you'd be wedded to the factory. Don't you think there'll be any sex in this marriage of yours?'

Even in the shadow she was held pinned by the fierceness in his voice.

'You couldn't even sit still a moment ago when I touched you, woman. You can't give up your life like that!'

'I can do anything I please so long as it doesn't hurt anybody else. My marriage would concern only my husband and myself,' Trudi snapped. She wished this man with his overwhelming sensuality was on the shore, and that he had not come swimming out to keep her company. The fact that he had prepared so carefully had impressed her. The food, the dry clothes would have been a life-saver if she had needed them. It annoyed her to think that he had bothered to search for her and possibly endangered his own life. She did not have to study his face, he would be wearing that same arrogant 'know it all' expression she despised.

Trudi stood up too.

'What does it matter to you? You're nobody to me, Dan Johnson.'

'Your name should be Circe,' he told her. 'If I hadn't seen you playing so happily at the creek, talked to you in the moonlight and seen your dance on the beach I wouldn't care, but that revealed someone else. That nereid was beautiful, she was a creature of love, a gentle girl, passionate music to the soul. I fell in love with that woman, I think.' His voice had become soft, almost tender.

'She doesn't exist, it was a whimsy of the moonlight,' Trudi said shortly. It was too dangerous standing taut beside him, and when he turned his head to study her she sat down abruptly. To her surprise Dan sat beside her again, and the touch of his thigh against hers set her pulses racing. Instinctively she moved away, but he simply pulled her closer, wrapping the rug over her.

'She's a dream woman, beautiful in the moonlight, yet mysterious. I wanted to make love to her, to cherish her, to protect her, to see her smile.' He moved slightly and Trudi felt his arm slip around her, turning her face to his.

His mouth claimed hers with infinite gentleness. Trudi felt herself respond to the mood he had spoken of and for a few moment she dared to hope that perhaps the world of love he had shone before her might have some hope. Their kiss seemed to lift them both to the stars, and she answered him, the sound of the sea crashing like the barriers around her heart.

'My beautiful nereid,' he whispered softly, as his finger found her ear. He bent and kissed it softly. He was exultant, and she felt his joy crash through her as he claimed her mouth yet again.

CHAPTER FOUR

'I won't ever stop loving you, my gift from the sea. You'll be the happiest woman in the land, I'll give you the moon and the stars and surround you with sunshine.'

For a few intoxicating moments Trudi let herself be carried away by Dan's words. It was heaven to be in his arms and she knew she had never experienced kisses such as those they had shared. Her body was a wild thing wanting his caresses and his gentle yet firm touch had promised so much.

She pushed him away and hid her face in her hands. She felt as if her body was being split. Could she risk loving? This man was a stranger. All she knew was so little—he rode a horse, he cleaned up the camp, he was a strong swimmer and he had read at some time in his life.

'I'll give you a little time, I've waited all my life for you to come along, my sea woman.' He was smiling, and Trudi gazed at him, trying to see his face.

'Sweetheart, we can reach stars together.'

He held her hand and blew a kiss on to her palm, closing the fingers over the spot as if to trap the kiss, then turned her head to the stars.

'Look at the bright star, Acheron—he almost seemed to be shining just for us. Even the Southern Cross is blazing tonight. My love is as constant as those paths, my nereid,' he whispered.

'Please, I can't take any more,' gasped Trudi.

It was true. It was bad enough that the man's body

should be so physically attractive, but she would have no defences left if his mind continued to delight her. She knew without being told that Dan was baring a side that few others would have seen. It touched her deeply, and she knew too that her instincts were screaming at her that this was right, that this was a man she could be happy with for ever.

He held her quietly, looking at her. 'Have some coffee, Trudi.'

She took it, grateful for the drink, then choked in surprise.

Dan grinned. 'Sorry, nereid. I laced it before I came, I didn't know whether you'd be half frozen or not. It's good, though.' Again the smile flashed and she saw the white straight teeth in the faint light. She realised it had been growing lighter and she listened to the sea thinking that it didn't sound half as fierce as before. Quietly she passed him more of the coffee, then stood up and peered down.

'I think we can get down. There's hardly any sea, and you have the torch.'

'You're right, of course. I was hoping you'd believe me about being too dark to see. In half an hour it will be a little lighter and the rock will be surrounded by sand and we can get down. We might as well finish the coffee and be comfortable.'

Trudi frowned, supposing he was right. She would have liked to have confirmed her observations with the torch, but he had packed it in the bag beside him and she didn't want to lean over him. If he held her and kissed her again the madness might recur. The coffee was delicious and she sipped it slowly, thinking about the man beside her.

Dan suited him in some way, yet Daniel had a dignity that would match him better, she thought. His hands were tough and muscular, yet they had held her with sensitivity. Hands that could point to the stars but little else, she mused. Her thoughts raced pellmell.

'You think too much,' he whispered softly in her ear, and she felt again the quickening of her body as he curved her against him. She reached her arms around his neck unable to resist, wanting the fire of his kisses. Tantalisingly he kissed her briefly, then began to kiss her ear, her throat, her eyes before returning to her lips. Trudi felt the heavens were spinning as she felt the fathomless deep of that kiss. It had been much more than a brief physical exploration. Somewhere in it she had let Dan take control, and she shivered once he released her. For better or worse she was in love with this tender giant whom she had feared so intensely. She realised that she had been instinctively attracted to him right from the start.

'Trudi Carr, I'm in love with you. Will you marry me?'

'Stop joking about things like that, Dan Johnson!' Trudi spoke indignantly.

'I'm not joking, my nereid.' He stroked her hair, then bent to kiss her again. Despite herself Trudi felt the same swift rise of passion, and the lean hardness of his body made her aware of her own feelings.

She rolled away, determined that she had to fight the insane desire to love him. 'You're crazy, Dan Johnson! If it's any consolation I'm crazy too. It must be this wretched rock or the moonlight on the sea. Tomorrow we'll have forgotten all this nonsense.'

Dan lifted a curl from her ear so he could nibble it gently. His touch was delicate and Trudi gasped as the physical sensations flooded her.

'My nereid, I don't think you've got a chance of forgetting me, perhaps as much chance as that tide has of not turning. I've been waiting for someone like you all my life. I knew the minute you got rid of your chaperone that you would come to me.'

'Why, you conceited ape!' Trudi found all her tender feelings had dissolved in fury. 'I stayed on here because I liked it, not because of you.'

'Methinks the lady doth protest too much. Incidentally, there's a forfeit for that insult.' Smoothly he took her in his arms, ignoring her struggles, pushing her arms back, awaking the same mountainous feelings so that she felt her response in almost despair. 'I'll give you the moon and stars, my nereid,' he whispered as he cradled her lovingly, completely the master.

'I don't want the moon and stars. I'll thank you to leave Acheron and the rest of them exactly where they are!'

'Don't fight me, Trudi.' His voice was low and his eyes serious.

Trudi looked at him, her feelings storm tossed by her emotions. She had to admit Dan was right, she had known he was dangerous the minute she saw him. They were aware of the attraction between them. But that was all it was, she reminded herself. Dan was just a healthy male stuck in isolation with a female, she told herself tartly. She didn't dare to trust again.

'Trudi Carr, I'm in love with you. Will you marry me?'

Trudi gasped, realising that Dan had deliberately repeated the question.

'You hardly know me! I told you, I'm a career girl. I'm not interested in love and marriage.'

'But that was before you knew me,' said Dan, apparently not a whit abashed at her reply. 'You can't resist me, Trudi, even if you wanted to.'

He held her lightly and bent his mouth to hers. It

was a feather of a kiss, so fleeting that Trudi hardly felt it. Even so it caused her to move swiftly, and Dan pulled her back into the hollow of his arms with a soft mocking laugh.

'Leave me alone or I'll scream!' warned Trudi.

'You can scream, darling. Of course no one will hear you, this rock is in the ocean, remember. Besides, what would be the point? You're an intelligent young woman and you'll soon realise that I'm the one man to make you change your mind. You're a fraud as a Women's Libber, my sweet one.'

Very gently he lifted a dark strand of her hair from her ear and bent his body so that he could again nibble the tender pink shell. Trudi wriggled, unwilling to admit that Dan could be right. She was experiencing sensations of fire that lit her body.

'Try screaming, sweetheart, or haven't you any breath left?' he whispered, his eyes agleam.

Trudi opened her mouth, but no voice came. Dan reached over and touched her mouth with his lips, kissing her long and hard, and the stars suddenly zoomed in the sky. Trudi felt her arms creep around his back, loving the strength and firmness and the closeness of his body. She knew her mouth was saying ridiculous things, but it no longer seemed to matter. Instinctively she knew she could trust Dan Johnson. She sighed softly and Dan's head bent and dropped another feather-light kiss on her mouth.

'My woman of the stars,' he whispered. 'I love you, and you love me.'

'You're star-struck,' she whispered brokenly, struggling to sit up, but the strong arms merely tucked her back again before punishing her for her words with a devasting kiss.

'Oh, Dan!' she whispered at last.

'You're beautiful in defeat, my sweet one.' Dan wound a curl of her hair round his fingers. 'See, that's what you've done to me, wrapped yourself round my heart, so I can never be free.' He held her face in his hands for a moment, then ran his finger around the outline of her face. 'Your face is full of starshine, my love.'

'Dan, I'm not a moon and stars creature. Are you sure?'

'Of course! But you're a practical woman too, and although I can't give you a factory or two I can offer a good life at Ti Kouka.'

'I'm not saying I'm marrying you,' put in Trudi weakly.

'Don't worry, darling, I'll wait.'

'That'll be the day!' Trudi retorted with a touch of hauteur that collapsed under Dan's swift kiss to her neck.

'It's almost dawn, my fascinating siren.'

Together they watched the first pearl-grey light the edge of the eastern sky.

'Trudi, I'll see if we can get down,' said Dan, 'otherwise we might be here for another tide, and I could think of more comfortable places to be!'

A moment later he returned and held out his hand. Trudi found herself giving it and knew that Dan found it symbolic too as he kissed each fingertip in turn.

She trembled a little finding the fires in her body flaming. Dan seemed to understand as he held her quietly, his arm protective around her.

'We'll leave the gear here and I'll pick it up in daylight.' With his hand supporting her Trudi scrambled down the rock. The water was just splashing about the base of the rock, but she could step over it. However, Dan picked her up before she could get her feet wet and she slipped into his arms. He carried her back to the shore and put her down gently.

'Darling, come home with me to Ti Kouka. You'll love it.'

'Arrive on a place like Ti Kouka at three o'clock in the morning? Dan, have some sense. You'd wake everyone up.'

'They won't mind.'

Trudi shook her head firmly. Away from the magnetism of his touch her senses had returned. She tossed her hair back wearily. If she was going to meet his employers she wanted to do it wearing one of her best suits, her hair done and her make-up perfect.

'I'm vain, Dan! I want them to like me. They'll think I'm a bit of driftwood the tide brought in if they see me at the moment, and I don't want to make a bad impression.'

'My nereid, you couldn't make a bad impression if you tried. You look so utterly beautiful with your eyes like stars sparkling with love. But if you want to go back to the tent, your wish is my command!' He gestured with a mocking bow towards the truck parked on the roadside. 'Hardly the Golden Coach, darling, but more suitable for the beach. Hop in.' He gave her a helping shove and she flew up into the high seat. Dan clambered in and shut the door with a resounding bang. The keys swung gently in the ignition and she faced him with sudden perception.

'You could have had me off that island hours ago!' she accused.

'Yes. But I couldn't resist forcing you to stay in my company. I felt deep inside me that if we could only have a little time together you'd begin to trust me.' He chuckled as he brushed her hair back from her face.

'How did you find me?' she asked. 'How did you know I was missing?'

'I wasn't certain if you would deliberately stand me up or not in the afternoon, so I wasn't too surprised when you didn't show. I went for a swim, then I hiked off home. When I finished there I returned for the camp cleaning and I could see those pretty things of yours still floating on the line, so I knew you'd been away for some hours. I started worrying, but one of the campers mentioned you trotting off with your gear and gave me the direction, so I just followed your trail. Every so often it would disappear where the tide had covered your footsteps, but I kept casting forward trying to work out what you'd make for. I remembered the island. You were singing *Strawberry Fair*—I could just catch the odd bits between the waves! I couldn't figure out why you hadn't left earlier, so I prepared just in case.'

Trudi nodded, as Dan started the engine and the truck bumped across the uneven ground. She told him laughingly what she thought of the road.

'Just for you, I'll see what I can do! It really started as the farm swimming spot but just grew. We still get a few old hands who always return.'

'Would you come back here if you had to leave Ti Kouka?' she asked him. 'It's such a beautiful place.'

'Trudi, I'll never leave here. They'll cart me out head first. This is my life.'

Trudi nodded her head soberly. She felt a little rise of panic at the thought of always living in someone else's place, of being constantly careful with someone else's property, but then reminded herself that it wouldn't affect her.

The road passed over the ford and she was jostled about and it seemed to emphasise her predicament. She wanted to bend to this man and make room not only for him but this land he loved too, and it was a harsh, frightening place at times. The campsite seemed a relief, a sanctuary which would shelter her and keep her safe. Dan cut the motor and let the truck roll towards the entrance.

'Don't want to wake anyone,' he explained. 'We'll leave the truck here and walk in the rest. You're not too tired?'

'No, I'm fine, but I must admit I'm feeling a bit stiff and sore. I guess the rocks would be more comfortable with a chaise-longue installed!'

'I'll remember that!' he smiled. He lifted her down from the cab and as she slipped into his arms the touch of his body shook her awake. He held her tightly for a moment, then kissed her hard and passionately, so that her senses sped and she staggered against him.

'Darling, you're exhausted—I'm sorry. Go to bed and I'll see you tomorrow.' He watched as she crawled into her tent and then was gone. A few seconds later she heard the faint sound of the truck. She felt filthy and scratched and tired, but her whole being shivered with excitement. Her lips tingled still after the last heady kiss and she wondered again at the strange man she was afraid to love.

With the body of an athlete, he was a hard-working hobo totally without ambition, content with what he had; a passionate, arrogant male, persuasive and well read; and a questioning, observant farmer. There was a paradox somewhere, but Trudi was too tired to sort it out. She lay back, glad of the thick foam sheet she rested on. It was heaven, and she snuggled in, thinking how such a short time earlier she had snuggled against Dan. The memory sent her to sleep with a smile.

The sun was high when she woke at last, and she stretched happily. It took her a few moments to wonder why she felt so alive, then her lips met in a joyful curve as she remembered. For an instant she wondered if the whole incident had been a dream, but her missing rucksack and rug proved its reality. As she dressed she wondered about the time. She had forgotten to wind her watch the night before and there didn't seem to be much point in asking anyone now. She wished she knew what time Dan would come, sure he would visit her.

The sun shimmered on the white cliffs and she began preparing the fire. Someone had dumped a lot of dry firewood ready for her and she wondered if Dan had already been and seeing she slept, left her to rest. She sighed softly, wishing he had woken her.

The water was soon boiling, so she made some tea. She decided to cook a meal. It was quite delicious and she made surprisingly short work of it.

As she was clearing away, a couple of young children peeped up at her and realising she was the object of their scrutiny, Trudi began singing, making up the words to a tune they would know. It was all about a mermaid and a wicked chief, and the children crept closer to listen. By the time they had joined her on the plank, they were listening wide-eyed. At the end their smiles delighted her.

'You made that up,' said the tow-headed lad accusingly.

'No, she didn't,' put in his younger sister.

The children told her that they came to Bell Bay regularly, as their father was a friend of Sheridan Jay of Ti Kouka.

'Dad used to work for him, then he went to another farm, then he bought a business in town. He wanted to buy a farm, but he couldn't afford it,' the boy explained regretfully. 'So we come here and Dad helps in the holidays.'

'I think that sounds sensible,' put in Trudi soberly. She continued talking to the children and when their mother came along shortly afterwards, she enjoyed their brief conversation.

After they had departed she wandered down the sand, but not before she found that it was two o'clock.

She decided to visit her island prison to pick up her gear as an excuse to meet Dan. He would be bound to appear around two-thirty when the tide was lowest. Surely they could share a couple of minutes before he went back to his work, she thought.

Excitedly she ran a comb through her hair and put on lipstick, doing so in the car's mirror. Realising she wouldn't have time to walk there, she flicked the car keys into place. As she bounced along the track she saw that the children she had spoken to earlier had been joined by some others. Grinning, she waved back, reflecting on catching a glimpse of herself in the mirror, that she looked totally different. Hastily she pushed the mirror back into position and concentrated on driving. She didn't want Dan to have to rescue her from another awkward situation.

The long tramp was made in minutes, the longest part being in reaching the rocks from the road. She didn't want to take her beautiful car off the track, so she made three or four trips across the sands. She was just struggling back with the last load when the truck pulled up. Smiling, she stood waiting, then felt absurdly disappointed when Dan's figure did not leap out. Instead an older man jumped down agilely and gave her a welcoming smile.

'Reckon you're Trudi!' He held out a rough, work-hardened hand and shook hers. 'Mighty pleased to meet you. The name's Dave Forrest.'

His evident sincere warmth left Trudi in no doubt that this man knew she held a very special place in Dan's heart. Her smile was slightly nervous; she hadn't expected to meet Dan's friends and workmates wearing a skimpy top and matching shorts.

Dave Forrest's shrewd blue eyes met hers and he smiled, obviously reading her thoughts. 'Dan had to go to a meeting this afternoon. He'll be back later to see you. I said I'd pick the gear up for him and explain.'

Trudi helped him to pile the wet-suit and thermos flasks into the truck.

'Did you bring the other vehicle last night?' she enquired.

'Yes. 'Tisn't the first time Dan's been stuck there. Happened when he was seven, and his father nearly ate him! Fair little beggar he was for climbing and exploring. Never knew where he'd be next. He had his dog with him for company that time, reckon he did better last night!'

Trudi couldn't help her chuckle. It was interesting to hear about Dan as a small boy. Somehow he was so big, and manly, it seemed hard to picture him as a child.

'You must have been at Ti Kouka a long time?' she asked.

'Only place!' the man returned simply. 'I've lived here since I was fifteen. I don't ever think about anywhere else. This is home.'

'It's very beautiful,' admitted Trudi, looking along the rugged coastline.

'Wait till you see Ti Kouka! Tell you what, come and have a look now. A cup of tea would be good.'

Trudi felt embarrassed. 'I'm sorry, Mr Forrest, I don't really think I should go without Dan.' She smiled, indicating her outfit. 'I may look all right for the beach, but I'm certainly not dressed for calling.'

'You look just right, Trudi, but reckon Dan would want to take you himself. It's his place fair enough.'

'Are there a lot at Ti Kouka?'

'No. We hire extra labour when we need it. First there's Jay himself. Then his mother, Mrs Jay, lives there, but she's often at her town house in Christchurch; it hasn't been the same for her since the old man died. The shepherd and his wife live in one wing.

'My wife Anne and I have the bungalow. Anne's in town with the two eldest boys, getting them organised for boarding school again. How about coming to visit us? Anne will be back tomorrow night, so get Dan to bring you the next day.'

Trudi acquiesced with only a faint misgiving that events were running faster than she had allowed. Dave's comments showed that Dan had grown up on Ti Kouka. Evidently Dan's father had worked there most of his life too. It made her realise that she knew nothing of Dan's family and whether he had brothers or sisters. Dave Forrest would know, of course.

He looked at her with a smile.

'Tell me about Dan when he was small.'

Dave Forrest leaned against the truck, his eyes following a black and white dog running about on the sand.

'Whenever I think of Dan then I always see him with a dog like Rob running at his heels—on the go the whole time. He'd follow the boss like a shadow all over the farm. When he was tiny the boss would have him up front on the horse and he'd be trying to whistle to the dogs. Funniest thing to see. He always knew exactly what he wanted, determined and as stubborn

as the old man, straight as a totara tree. A just man.'
He paused and looked at Trudi shrewdly. 'You won't
ever have to worry about Dan.'

Trudi smiled. There was something very reassuring
about Dave Forrest.

'I hardly know Dan, but I know he's special,' she
put in, oddly shy.

'You'll be all right. You won't want for anything, of
course—Ti Kouka will see to that.'

'Dan loves it. He said he'd leave here carted out in a
box.'

'Of course. Same as me. I guess no one would really
understand until they lived here and put down roots.
There's room to grow here.'

'How does Dan get on with Mrs Jay? Is she so
dreadful?'

'Well now, Dan will take you along to meet the
tyrant and you'll be able to form your own opinion.'
Dave Forrest smiled. 'Don't worry, Sheridan Jay is
the apple of her eye, so you've no problems.'

Thinking this over Trudi agreed. The boss's mother,
although interested, would hardly be personally
affected by Dan's girl-friend. After all, it wasn't her
son. This made her realise that she knew little of Dan's
mother. Dave hadn't mentioned her. Still, she could
hardly interrogate Dave Forrest.

'I guess I'll meet everyone sooner or later. After all,
I've really only just met Dan.'

'Yeah, and I better get my work done or the boss
will wonder what's happened! My two youngest, Robin
and Angela, are playing down at Bell Bay with some
friends. You might see them there.'

He stepped to the truck and pursed his lips to emit
the loudest shrillest whistle which Trudi had ever
heard. Its effect was instantaneous. The dog, far out

on the sands, stopped and looked up sharply, then ran towards them, its paws flicking sand as it sped along the beach. With practised ease it jumped on to the tray of the truck and stood there, its plume of a tail wagging happily.

Trudi waved goodbye as the truck was edged out and turned back towards Ti Kouka. She folded the rug neatly and put it into the car, her thoughts puzzled. Dave Forrest could tell her so much about Dan and she knew so little. Dan hadn't mentioned his mother; where was she? Was she alive? Had she abandoned Dan? Had she found the isolation of Ti Kouka too much and returned to the city? Could that explain why Dan had spoken so warmly of Mrs Jay, even if he cheekily referred to her as a tyrant? The nickname was evidently familiar, from Dave's comments.

She drove down the track, glad that she had met and liked Dave Forrest. He seemed to love Ti Kouka just as devotedly as Dan.

The thought came to her that Dan's wife would be under constant supervision living at the homestead. It would be bad enough living in someone else's house, but to have a tyrant living there too, her husband's boss, another couple and possibly a mother-in-law, sounded a recipe for disaster.

Any children would have to be very quiet in the homestead, tiptoeing around for fear of the fierce old lady. If they made a noise life could be a misery. The tantalising image of a small boy like Dan tore at her, but then she pictured a sad-eyed little girl like herself, remembering the unhappy times since her father died. That was not the sort of existence she wanted for children or for herself, she admitted.

'Dan, I can't love you,' she muttered desperately. She had the feeling that she had been swept into the man's net as easily as the poor fish in the sea. If Dan would only leave Ti Kouka, they could always return for holidays, she thought with burgeoning hope.

The thought of a woman she had met and liked that morning hit her forcibly. Her family had compromised, and judging by the lavish caravan, their expensive car and the small boat, had succeeded. Trudi sighed. She couldn't see Dan leaving Ti Kouka. The look on his face when he looked over the land was full of pride— more, love. Trudi bit her lip as she tried to puzzle it out. The sound of the incoming tide reminded her that Dan should soon be back. Her heart was beating fast when the familiar jeep rolled up and to her disappointment Dave Forrest swung down. She watched as he removed the rubbish and then she went disconsolately back into her tent, not bothering with a fire. She didn't feel like food.

Watching the waves lap up against the sand was soothing and she began to wonder if she had made too much black of the whole picture. She sat waiting, sure that Dan would come.

It was late before she put away her things and went sadly to bed. Her thoughts troubled her. She sighed, thinking about Dan and how he had held her in his arms. So much for his announcement that he loved her and wanted to marry her! she thought. Angrily she thumped her pillow and tried to sleep. She wondered why she felt so ridiculously hurt.

The following morning she walked through the bush and out to the top of the cliffs. She wore her backpack so she would not forget her drink bottle. She reached the spot where she and Maria had lunched such a short time before, and sat down. It was still early and the song of the birds delighted her, hearing the bellbirds' mellifluous tones and the throaty chuckle and rasp of the tui, quickly changing to an imitation of the bellbird, amused her. She looked carefully but couldn't see the tuis for some time. Finally she caught sight of the pair, and watched as the sunlight made a rainbow sheen of the black of their wings. The heavy beat of their wings, as they were surprised, startled her. The sound of a horse coming purposefully along the track revealed the answer. She felt her heart speed up as Dan turned a corner.

'I've been looking for you, darling,' he called. 'Sorry it was too late to come last night, but I knew you would understand I had to work.'

'It's all right,' Trudi answered, blithely ignoring the thousands of questions and doubts his absence had inspired.

'How did you find me?'

He chuckled. 'I'll always know where to find you, darling, if you're on Ti Kouka. I checked the camp and when I found you weren't there, the birds told me someone was up here, so I came after you.' He smiled his lovely wide smile which was so very special, and Trudi could no resist smiling back.

'You're the most beautiful creature in the world, my Trudi could not resist smiling back.

'I'm not your Trudi,' she denied, but at his touch she felt her limbs melt.

'Not yet, but soon,' he said softly, completely confident of his powers of persuasion. 'You were making for the top?' He pointed to the summit of the cliffs a couple of miles away.

'Yes. I saw you up there the first day we arrived and both Maria and I were fascinated. I'm sure there would be a great view from there.'

'Just about all of Ti Kouka and a whole lot of coastline too,' he answered. 'I'll leave the horse here and we can go together.' He looped the reins up out of the way and spoke to the horse quietly and softly. Two dogs had approached Trudi before and now she patted them. Both were sleek working dogs and she guessed huntaways would be very necessary on the farm.

Dan slipped his arm around her and shouldered the back-pack. A short whistle brought both dogs up and they set off together. Dan held Trudi's arm loosely, occasionally using the binoculars to check the distant paddocks. He held them out for her to view and she jumped back as the cliff top swung into shape immediately before her eyes. She was staggered at the clarity of the detail.

'You can see everything!' she exclaimed.

'Even a naughty lady poking out a saucy tongue,' he countered, 'or a mermaid in a pool.' His eyes danced merrily. 'I thought it was so hot, I was seeing a mirage. I knew the creek was real, though, and I couldn't resist going to check. There was a beautiful woman with dark hair and a magnificent body.' He teased with a lightning smile. 'It took me a moment to realise the car and your sister were there too. By the time I reached you, the pair of you were playing like young colts. And then you looked at me as though I was something the cat had dragged in. And I saw your hair was brown like your eyes and that you were proud and untamed as the wind, and I decided I had to know you.' Dan's voice was full of humour.

'Rubbish!' snorted Trudi inelegantly.

'Yes, I agree,' he chuckled. 'But it sounded better than saying I thought you were stupid to be travelling in such heat!'

They both laughed and looked at each other with love before walking on again. Trudi turned and looked back. Already the view was staggeringly beautiful, but

Dan promised her an even grander vista once they reached the top. The climb was getting steadily steeper, making her puff slightly, so Trudi was glad of Dan's strong arms at times. The muscles at the back of her legs protested and he taunted her with her lack of fitness, promising that once they married she would have plenty of exercise. This was said with such panache that Trudi abruptly dropped his arm, only to have it seized again. She was glad as the last few feet were extremely difficult.

He pulled her up and they stood together. Below, the cliffs fell steeply to the sea, but on the other side they eased and sloped more gently down to the hidden bay. The water appeared more green than blue and rocks littered the entrance. The sweep of the coastline was blurred as the curve merged in the distance with the sea. The long pale band of shore was mirrored by a similar line to the south. Dan turned her inland, and she gasped at the vivid beauty before her. Through a gap she could see the rich lands of the valley lying like some other world protected behind the huge sleeping hills. In the distance she could see the main homestead and to one side the bungalow, both sheltered by their trees. The fields were gold and green and brown in a sunlit shaft of colour, and she didn't need to be an expert to realise the fertility of the land lying spread before her.

'Ti Kouka!'.

Dan's love was measured in the reverence with which he spoke the word. Seeing it from this angle, Trudi felt a stir of panic and wondered if she would ever mean more to Dan than this land.

CHAPTER FIVE

'It's so vast—I'd no idea!'

'Look, Trudi, see those cabbage trees at the end of this ridge? The original Sheridan J.S.T. Jay climbed up here, along the same route as we came and saw this valley. He made his way back hotfoot to buy it, and was very nearly accused of madness in wanting such a spot. They advised him to take a block lower down, but he insisted and registered it. Of course, there's a lot of land that has to be kept as a barrier, and always will, but there's more than enough to lead a good life at Ti Kouka.'

'You wouldn't ever leave here and buy somewhere else?'

He turned to her in genuine puzzlement. 'Leave Ti Kouka? Buy somewhere else? Don't be daft, woman!'

Trudi could not doubt his reply and her heart lurched painfully. She supposed the desire for her own home was a little feeble viewed by Dan's non-commercial standard. Oddly he evidently admired the perspicacity of the first Sheridan J.S.T. Jay, whom the present occupant had been named after. The whole place seemed rather like a benevolent feudal society, she thought sourly, Dan was so pleased to be there that he asked for little else.

'That's why he called it Ti Kouka—it's Maori for cabbage trees. He'd been going along the coast stopping and checking from the hills along the way, for land. He'd make for the highest point. Those cabbage trees are clearly visible out to sea. He said he'd climb to the *ti kouka* or give up, and as he'd been celebrating his birthday the night before, he nearly did. Each step as he went up the hill at the end he muttered '*ti kouka*', so that's how the homestead was named.' Dan's grin was so wide she didn't know if he was serious or not. He carried on, gesturing. 'He went down the other way, naturally enough.'

Her eyes widened as Dan pointed out other features and she leaned against him. The wind played softly with her hair, blowing a tendril across Dan's face, and he removed it gently then kissed her.

'I want you to love Ti Kouka, my enchantress. You'll love Mrs Jay. She's not too bad for a tyrant!' He spoke warmly, but Trudi felt chilled. She was glad that Dan was looking over the land so he didn't see the expression on her face.

'Ti Kouka's an old place and full of character. I can just imagine you walking down the stairs,' he went on.

Trudi frowned. She didn't want Dan drawing more pictures, he was too hard to resist. She sat up, and the movement made her conscious of the tiny fuzz on Dan's chest. She tickled him and his answer was swift. 'My tantalising woman, we'd better move or you'll get burnt!'

Trudi moved. She knew Dan didn't mean sunburn and she recognised the levels at which they had arrived so speedily.

'So sensible!' she muttered softly.

'We'll have lunch under the trees—I hope you packed enough?'

'Oh, Dan, you'll have to tighten your belt a little, I'm afraid.'

For answer he smiled and wound his finger through her hair.

'Round my heart.' He spoke quietly and then

gathered her close so that her head rested on his chest. Infinitely slowly he turned her so that she was facing him, aware of his masculine magnetism and the faint tang of his aftershave. The touch of his hands triggered a response and she lifted her lips. His kiss was gentle and sweet and she swayed close, feeling the love surround her.

'My nereid, I love you.'

The kiss seemed to reach from the earth to the sky, joining them for ever. Trudi reeled back, all her senses clamouring. Free, she ran suddenly to avoid him seeing the pleasure his caress had given. She reached the safety of the trees and sat against a fallen log, the sound of the leaves soughing gently above. The topknot of trees formed a deep open square and they sheltered in the middle. To Trudi's surprise Dan proceeded to bring forth an extraordinary array from the back-pack.

'How did that get there?' she asked, as a bottle of champagne joined the rest.

'I put it there, of course. You were making friends with the dogs, so it was simple enough to slip it all in.'

It was fun, admitted Trudi, sitting on top of the world, every aspect unclouded. They shared a chicken Dan had broken up and pulled the wishbone together, then were both delighted when it broke equally.

'Guess we both wished for the same thing, Trudi,' said Dan as he reached for her. His firm well cut mouth whispered words of love and she could not help her own excitement, loving the feel of his firm muscular body emphasised by his working clothes of light shirt and shorts. She could hear the sound of his heart when she laid her head against his chest. There was such joy in lying in his arms and she turned, meeting his kiss.

'Darling, we belong together,' he said softly. 'It's never been like this before. I want to know everything about you, from the top of your head to those painted toenails of yours, especially why one foot is painted pink and the other red!'

'Dan, I'll never know when you're being serious,' she chuckled as she touched the firm lines of his shoulder, noting the way the frame was built so powerfully. 'Well, the saga of the toes is simple. I started to change it this morning and was doing so when I was interrupted and then I forgot.'

She lay contentedly in his arms, seeing the crinkle of the laughter lines around his eyes, oddly white in his deep tan. She traced the edge of his mouth with her fingertip and he lay looking at her, then moved to take her finger and kiss it gently.

'Trudi, I love you, I don't want to ever do anything to hurt you. Neither of us wants a hothouse type relationship, a brief flowering, then dead.' He regarded her so seriously, then the mood lightened as he smiled.

Trudi took a long look around, soaking up every aspect. Even the clouds which seemed to have built up farther to the south seemed a part of the beauty, emphasising the dark shadows from which she had come to the sunlit land in front of her. Suddenly she knew Dan was right. She had to love him, because without him life held little joy.

'I love you,' she said quietly, and saw his face hold the sunshine itself.

Their kiss was very deep. Together they walked slowly down from the hill. Dan escorted her back through the bush, and the trip was a delight. Standing softly in one spot, he mimicked the call of the bellbirds and Trudi was delighted to hear first one bird and then another answer. Gradually there seemed to be a

whole merry peal of softly pitched notes as more
bellbirds came to investigate. It took Trudi a few
moments to see a small green bird sitting poised amid
the leaves and then a swift scurry as two more
appeared. It was her swift gasp of pleasure that
sent the birds flying away and she felt suddenly
bereft.

'Don't worry, darling, they'll come again another
time, you'll have to learn their call. This is Bell Bay,
after all.'

'Old Sheridan, whatever his name, was scarcely
original,' she said, smiling, and Dan nodded.

'The birds have these hills, as we like to keep it more
or less as a sanctuary, but this section is needed as a
short cut. Farther over, past the camp, it's really
rugged country and there are more birds there.
Unfortunately more wildcats too that I'll have to deal
with. I've even seen a kiwi there years ago, but I'm not
sure if there are any left now.'

'Could we go looking one day? I realise you have to
work, but you must get some time off.' Trudi smiled,
pointing an admonitory finger. 'You're dreadful, you
should be working, not slacking around with your
girl.'

'Right, boss,' he said, and his eyes twinkled.

The horse followed behind and the sounds of the
two dogs forging ahead echoed as they went on down
the path. At the stile Dan held her and kissed her again
before he turned and mounted the horse, and Trudi
watched as he rode off along the fenceline leading back
to Ti Kouka. In a whirl of happiness she waltzed down
the track and out on to the camping ground. The sky
seemed more blue, the beach more magnificent, the
whole world more wonderful than ever.

'Much more of Dan Johnson, Trudi Carr,' she

muttered, 'and folks will be calling you the Cheshire Cat!'

Dreamily she wandered off towards the beach; seeing the driftwood and remembering her attempts at carving, she looked around for others. After a while she pounced on one which made her face light up. Happily she viewed it from all angles, then picked up some sticks for burning and set off back to the camp. From time to time she cast a glance towards the clifftops, but there was no sign of any familiar rider. She hoped Dan wouldn't get into trouble for being late back, then she remembered the picnic. Obviously his employer knew about the girl at the camping ground. Idly she wondered what Sheridan Jay was like. She would hardly have made a good impression taking one of his junior employees away from his work.

She had liked Dave Forrest, she reminded herself. He hadn't said much about the big boss, she remembered, possibly he believed in people forming their own opinions.

The beach drove the worrying thoughts of her future husband's employer out of her mind. The children were already swimming and she joined them, meeting Dave Forrest's two youngest at the same time. The children explained that their father was busy helping S. Jay, and Trudy felt guilty again. With relief she remembered the long hours Dan had spent for his employer the previous day.

Afterwards they lay on the sand, and it was only as the sun dropped that she realised that Dan would visit the camp again to remove the rubbish and clean the place. Hastily she said goodbye to her friends, then sped off down the shore. She ran past Rangitira, noticing automatically that his head was covered, and realised that she was becoming more conscious of the tides and their movements.

Her smile drooped comically when she saw the truck at Bell Bay and could make out Dave Forrest. She changed from her sticky suit and began to cook a light tea. She lit the fire for a drink of tea as she was sure that Dave would wander down and she wanted to be able to offer him a cup. Her friends had returned and the Forrest children had rejoined their father and were helping too.

The fire was crackling well, so she edged her pots forwards. With the aroma of food she found that she was hungry and when she had completed her meal the tight awareness of her shorts decided her that her holiday was doing her too much good.

She had just cleared away the meal when Dave Forrest dropped by and he had a drink of tea. Listening to his tales of earlier times at Ti Kouka was fascinating. The children were tired, though, so he reminded Trudi about visiting them the following afternoon with Dan, then left.

After waving goodbye she fossicked around till she found the piece of wood she had carefully selected earlier. The shape was quite clear and she felt sure that Dan would like it. The outline of the swaying cabbage tree was so familiar from Dan's horse blanket to the sign on the truck and jeep. No doubt at the homestead everything would have a similar design. He loved Ti Kouka so much, she felt sure the small carving would delight him.

Dave had told her that Dan wouldn't be down that night and she felt a little hurt, then chided herself for feeling that way. She wished she could have her hair done properly, before meeting Mrs Forrest. The cold water showers and salt swims hadn't improved its looks. Idly she puzzled over whether she would look very different if she had her hair cut short, and if Dan would approve.

She could almost hear Maria's voice saying, 'See, I told you once you fell in love you'd understand.' She grinned at herself and brushed her hair all the longer, thinking how she had changed since that first day at the creek. Then she hadn't even wanted to give the man a drink, now she wanted to share everything with him. As she lay in her sleeping bag she could admit that Dan had washed away all her bitterness and past disappointments. Life on Ti Kouka would hold its challenges and joys.

Trudi woke in the cool light of early dawn and walked over to the water tap with her bucket. A fisherman was busy cleaning the fish he had just caught and invited her to join his wife and himself for breakfast. She chatted as she was handed a welcome cup of tea. The couple told her they came each year for part of their holiday and spent the other part in Fiji, Tonga or the Cook group in winter. Trudi listened enviously as they spoke of different places, but they both agreed that Ti Kouka had a special charm. Again they seemed to like the wonderful Mr Jay enormously.

'Of course, Trudi, he's been everywhere,' the fisherman's wife commented. 'He's got a big responsibility in Ti Kouka, but he's got a great staff. Mind you, he works as hard as any of them.

'He's trying out some original ideas for farming too, as well. He's most interested in crop research and is doing some highly specialised studies in conjunction with the Lincoln University,' added the fisherman.

'Here's your breakfast, Trudi.'

Her nostrils had been aware of the aroma of fish cooking for some time, so she was prepared to see that the white flesh on her plate looked like the fish she ate at home. There the similarity ended. The meal was superb and Trudi decided that there was nothing quite so delicious as freshly caught fish, providing someone else did the catching!

She felt wonderfully relaxed and carefree and more than ever glad she had returned to Bell Bay. As she went through her morning routine she wondered if she would have ever met Dan again if she had not come back. The thought was at the back of her mind and she acknowledged that subconsciously she must have wanted to see him again. She hung up a polyester silky dress she had flung in at the last moment. It was a pretty pale pink turning to a dusky rose colour and she knew it suited her. She would wear it in the afternoon to meet Mrs Forrest. After setting her hair in a few clips, wishing she had such a civilised piece of equipment as a three-pin power plug to run her hair-dryer, she lay lazily on the warm grass soaking up the sunshine.

The sound of the truck coming along the road made her raise her head. Joyfully she recognised the jeep and saw Dan's distinctive large figure swing down.

She ran over to him and he kissed her, his hand immediately freeing the curl of hair she had clipped earlier.

'You have beautiful hair, Trudi,' he said softly. 'We're not expected at Dave and Anne's till later on, so I thought I'd take you round to Seal Bay. Put some old shoes on your feet, the rocks can be sharp.'

His eyes were gentle and Trudi smiled back at him, her breath catching as his hand held hers. He swung on a back-pack, announcing that they would have another picnic. They made their way over to the now familiar beach and followed the sand to the cliffs. Trudi could see that the tide had exposed the giant rocks at the base of the cliffs.

Dan climbed easily, checking her footsteps several times. She was glad, as with the spray flying towards them it was not a trip she would have liked to have tried on her own. When at last he released her hand she was relieved to see the golden sand again.

'Well done, Trudi,' Dan approved. 'It will be easier after lunch, when the tide is fully out. You'll have no difficulty then.'

Trudi felt as pleased as if she had been decorated. Dan's broad figure blocked her view and he smiled at her.

'Welcome to Seal Bay!'

He moved to lift her down the last rock and she gasped at the beauty. A tiny crescent bay lay before her, surrounded by enormous cliffs. Only a small strip of sand was in the centre, the rest rocky, with the wave spray forming a misty veil, pierced by a rainbow of light.

'Over here, Trudi.'

Gratefully Trudi followed Dan's lead. Stepping gingerly, she found herself on a small perch made from an old tree. Dan sat beside her and their eyes met in instant communication. Below and around them the sea met in an orchestra of sound. It took Dan's nod to divert her eyes towards the dark little blobs in the sea. A group of seals swam towards the rocks. With an awkward jump and a wriggle the first sleek black head peeped around and a moment later the other joined it.

Dan squeezed her hand in warning as two smaller shapes joined them. Each young seal was scarcely big enough to flipper their way up on to the rock, and Trudi bit back a sigh of relief when a larger wave gave them an extra push, sending them up safely. As they watched the seals play Dan told her the young would have been born in June or July. He pointed out their coats of olive grey covering a brown layer of thick underfur. The adults had much darker coats, and their sleek beauty as they dived and slid down the rocks delighted Trudi. One particularly venturesome pup slid towards them lifting his tiny black snout and wriggling his whiskers. His moist black eyes looked round for a moment, then he turned and lolloped his way back to the water. Where he had been awkward before, he now made them smile as he jumped and dived and cavorted, bullying the other pup into the game.

As they watched Dan handed her sandwiches and a thermos flask of tea. Conscious of the need for quiet, they scarcely spoke. At last Dan pointed to his watch and reluctantly they stood up. Instantly the seals dived into the water and their dark heads showed how swiftly they could move.

'Dan, that was a wonderful experience. How did you know?' she asked.

'They had to be,' he smiled. 'Everything has to be perfect for you, my true one.' Seeing her look, his smile became wider and he shook his head.

'Disbelieving woman! All right, I'll admit it. They're usually to be found in or near Seal Bay. From their point of view it's ideal. A boat would get smashed to pieces, unless it was loaded the same way we came, and I can't see anyone doing that with a load of sealskins. In the old days this would have been a natural sanctuary. And Sheridan Jay will see it remains one,' he ended.

'I'm glad,' said Trudi simply.

Dan helped her down and she bent and picked up a tiny green stone which caught her eye. She threw it to Dan and, laughing, he put it in her jacket pocket, telling her it was a present from Seal Bay.

'Why, thank you, kind sir. I shall treasure it as one

would the finest of diamonds,' she said with a smile, hiding the instant thought that poor Dan would hardly be likely to buy her such stones.

'And when you're seventy-five I'll ask for it,' he teased. 'So mind you keep it.'

'Oh, Dan, I love you!' she exclaimed.

'Of course, but it's nice you know it.'

'You conceited . . .! I'll . . . I'll . . .'

'Ssh, kiss me instead! 'Cause I love you.'

Trudi willingly put her arms around him, feeling the enchantment of his touch again as his mouth met hers in a long kiss. At last they looked at each other in deep seriousness and their hands locked together. There was something awe-inspiring about the moment, and Trudi knew instinctively that they would never forget it. This was a moment of pure love, they were both aware of a trust for each other.

Scrambling over the rocks was child's play now the tide was right out and soon they ran along the little curved beach together and back to the camp. Even as they slowed Trudi became aware of Dan's frown.

'What's wrong, Dan?' she asked.

'The shepherd's come down—it's probably a message. He hasn't been here long.'

'How on earth do you know that?'

'Elementary, my dear Watson! The truck's still got a damp patch on the side and on the tyres from the creek. Five minutes in this heat and it would have gone.'

Trudi's smile acknowledged and she released her hand from his.

'I'll go and get changed while you see him.'

'O.K., sweetheart.'

She veered away to her tent, her heart singing with happiness. She washed and brushed her hair, then changed into the pink dress, taking pains with her make-up for the first time since leaving the city. Then she went to Dan.

'A call from your boss, Mr Maugh,' he told her. 'He'd like you to consider going back to help. Apparently they have some big deal you were working on and the Australian buyer's flying over today. He said you can have a couple of weeks off later.'

'The Syd-Church deal? That's fantastic! If the man is coming to us we really do have a chance.' Trudi flung her arms round Dan. 'I've been sending this firm some of our material and designs and we've been close to pulling off a deal all December. Then over Christmas the whole thing flopped. I thought we'd missed the boat. Oh, Dan, this could be really big!' Her mind was humming with the exciting possibilities the new deal opened. 'Of course, we might not get it,' she cautioned, remembering some of their opposition. 'But I'll do my darned best. Oh, Dan! It's the end of my holiday for a while. Help me pack up?'

'Whoa! Not so fast, Trudi! Mr Maugh said he'd meet the guy and look after him today. You won't need to go till late tonight. There won't be any action till tomorrow.'

'Oh, Dan! I'll have to go like the wind to see that every detail is organised, this is too big to leave to maybe! If only I'd been at the office this week I'd have it all in order.'

She saw Dan's smile and laughed at her own enthusiasm.

'All right, you might think it's not important, but really it is to the factory.'

'Trudi, you look so pretty with your eyes sparkling. Don't forget the Forrests, though.'

Trudi thought rapidly. The boss knew how to deal with the situation, she admitted to herself. He'd been drawing up contracts for years, but this particular one she had conceived. She looked at the campsite and realised that it would take her a while to clear it, even beginning immediately. Courtesy demanded she keep her appointment with the Forrests.

'You're right, Dan. We can call on Mrs Forrest on my way out.'

'I'll help.'

Surprisingly it took little time to repack everything. She didn't have time to be nervous about meeting Mrs Forrest.

'You're beautiful,' Dan whispered as he kissed her very gently. 'I daren't make a mess of that make-up,' he grinned. 'I haven't seen you in your warpaint before. Darling, I'll follow you in a couple of minutes, so you won't have to eat all my dust.'

'Thanks, Dan. I'm glad you're coming with me.'

'You'll be fine, sweetheart. Just remember I love you.'

Trudi felt her eyes mist suddenly and she was glad Dan opened the door and she was forced to turn on the key and concentrate on driving. She was absurdly conscious of Dan's tall figure watching as she turned the car and headed out on to the beach road. This time she negotiated the track more expertly and seeing the dust cloud following her was glad of Dan's foresight. She turned into the bungalow's drive. It was set among trees, and Trudi loved it at first sight. It was a modern brick home and, from the roofline, quite large. Dave Forrest came out to meet her and she felt a flutter of nervousness, realising how important this meeting was to Dan, as well as herself. She parked the car and Dave came over to lead her towards the house. Dan's jeep rolled in beside her and he swung out easily, his hand clasping hers. Mrs Forrest waited by the steps, a smile on her face, and Trudi realised with surprise that the other woman was just as nervous of meeting her as she had been meeting them.

The introduction over, Trudi was shown into the lounge which had large ranch sliders out on to a terrace overlooking a lawn. She couldn't restrain a gasp of admiration at the scene in front of her.

'It's beautiful!' she exclaimed.

'We think so. Dave and I chose this spot only after a lot of thought.' She smiled at Dan, including him in the conversation. 'Even S. Jay thinks we couldn't have done better unless we moved to Ti Kouka point, and the prospect of climbing there is enough to put anyone off!'

'I've been there. Dan and I had a picnic. Great view, but oh, my muscles!' Trudi chuckled.

The ice was completely broken and they began to talk easily. Trudi felt relieved seeing the good humour that Dan and the Forrests shared. She felt herself welcomed with an open mind and was grateful that the Forrests were prepared to like her for Dan's sake. Anne told her about her first arrival on Ti Kouka and her meeting with Mrs Jay and Sheridan Jay. As she was about to question her hostess further on this all-important point, their conversation was interrupted by the children who pushed in a tea wagon, positioning it carefully. Evidently Mrs Forrest had taken great pains as the silver tea service and the fine bone china and the dainty cream cakes showed.

The children were obviously on their best behaviour and Trudi smiled, remembering the happy little beach urchins she had seen earlier. Both were very like their mother in appearance and Mrs Forrest explained that the two eldest ones were busy fixing up a fence, as the boys were anxious to earn some money of their own, and Sheridan Jay had promised to pay them. Smiling, Trudi agreed that it was a good idea to let the boys help, although it seemed tough on their holidays. She saw the swift flash that passed between Dan and Mr Forrest.

'Trudi, the boys have always helped out, that's how they learn to run the farm, the same way as Dave and I did. Sure they've got to go down to the city for high school, but I bet both boys would say that the real fun comes from working at Ti Kouka in the holidays.'

'I have to agree,' put in Anne. 'The boys think S. Jay is the greatest! He's subsidising a scheme to get them new bikes. Last year he helped them with a mechanics course and the equipment he set up in the garage is wonderful. I just wish more youngsters had the kind of life our children lead.'

'Anne, you sound like a commercial,' chuckled Dan. 'Give us a chance! We only met a few days ago.'

'Well, you never were one to let the grass grow where it shouldn't!' Anne riposted. 'I just want Trudi to know how happy she would be here.' She glanced towards her husband and he crinkled up his face into a myriad smile lines. Their joy was obvious.

'Where did you live before you built here?' queried Trudi.

'At Ti Kouka, of course. You haven't been there yet?'

'Dan wanted me to go at two o'clock the other morning, but I didn't think I looked my best.'

Both women chuckled and Trudi knew that she had found a friend.

'I remember my first introduction to the "tyrant". I was worried sick! There was no need, of course. For Dan's girl the welcome will be even warmer. I think Mrs Jay was beginning to think she had a bachelor on her hands, despite all the girls' efforts. Dave wondered the other day when Dan commented that he'd seen a mermaid in the creek. According to Dave you gave Dan the "get lost" treatment, and I think that must have been the first time anyone's done that to Dan. And to add insult, it was on Ti Kouka too!'

Looking at Dan, Trudi felt her colour rise. His eyes crinkled back at her with a teasing light.

'Was it? I thought the creek would have been council or public land.'

'No. Once you leave the tarseal at the fork you're on Ti Kouka property. It is a private road.'

She explained to Anne and Dave that she had been summoned back to the city for her work and they commiserated with her on the abrupt ending of her holiday. Anne told her that she was frequently in Christchurch to see the boys, and Trudi gave her the address and her telephone number and urged her to call.

Altogether it had been a most enjoyable visit, thought Trudi, as she went down the road. Behind her Dan was driving as he had promised to escort her to the road fork. Smiling that he was no doubt giving time for the dust to settle, she pulled up at the side of the road. It seemed only a short time to wait. She noticed then that someone, no doubt deliberately, had planted some of the cabbage trees by the fork, and absently she studied them. They were familiar to her from babyhood as there had been one in their garden at home, and she looked now at the straight trunk with its tufts of green sitting on top rather like flax bushes. The tree trunk was knobbly and slightly hairy and she rubbed it absently, thinking that until Dan had mentioned it she hadn't known the Maori name for the New Zealand cordyline been Ti Kouka. It was not one she would be likely to forget now, she thought. All the same, the early name of palm lily had been rather more mellifluous than cabbage tree. Dan had said he would cook her a dish of it some time, warning her that despite its name it was slightly bitter. Apparently many pioneers had been forced into eating it while waiting for their first crops to grow.

Dan coasted to a stop. 'You make a pretty picture waiting under the trees,' he teased.

'I was just thinking that you'd promised to cook me some.'

'Well, there are tastes I'd rather have,' he grinned. 'There's plenty of time, and lots of cabbage trees. There's so much to show you about Ti Kouka, Trudi. You haven't even come home with me yet.'

'I'm a bit scared of that, Dan. Can we leave it for a bit?'

'So long as it's not too long, Trudi. After all, what would frighten you? No sea monsters or taniwhas at Ti Kouka,' he smiled as he pulled her into his arms.

'I know I'll never be happy away from you now, but I can't help thinking that I don't really know you,' she confessed. 'I don't even know whether you've got sisters or brothers.'

'There's just me,' he smiled. 'Stop worrying!'

His kiss followed immediately, and again the loving firm pressure awoke the pounding of her blood. She nestled against him, content to feel the love wrapping around her. It was Dan who finally broke the embrace and pushed her none too gently to the car.

'You come to stay at Ti Kouka next weekend, Trudi. Once you've seen it you'll understand.'

'Yes, sir,' she answered with a smile.

Only as she finally pulled out on to the road did she realise she hadn't asked Dan about his mother. Going by the last comment she must live at Ti Kouka too. Or didn't she count in her only child's estimation? The latter thought was enough to make Trudi frown, as it seemed out of character with the man she loved. Thanks to Anne and Dave she knew a little more about Sheridan High and Mighty Jay. He evidently liked children and they liked him, which gave her some relief. Both Dave Forrest and Dan were not the types to work for a man they disliked. Trudi decided she would probably not have too much to worry about him, which left her with the hard-sounding woman whom evidently all, regardless of consequence, called 'tyrant'. Dan was right: the sooner she met her for herself the better.

Dave Forrest had said that for the 'tyrant', life at Ti Kouka hadn't been the same since the Old Man had died. That must have been when she had bought the flat in town where she spent quite a lot of time.

Anne Forrest had been able to live with the 'tyrant' and survive, Trudi consoled herself, but Anne was a farmer's daughter who was eminently suitable for her role. How would the 'tyrant' appreciate a career girl in her home, one who had never even stayed on a farm before? If the 'tyrant' did not approve, what effect would it have on her relationship with Dan?

CHAPTER SIX

THE entrance to Christchurch seemed to come with astonishing speed and Trudi was pleased with the smoothness of her trip. She went straight to the factory, and once there it took her only a few minutes to select the necessary papers, then she went back to her flat. She dialled Maria's number and heard the good humour in her sister's voice when she answered.

'Maria, I'm home!'

'Trudi!—I wasn't expecting you back just yet. I'm so pleased you rang. I've been longing to tell you our news. John's been promoted to Wellington, and we'll be shifting in five weeks.'

'Really? That's great! Congratulate John from me.'

'His firm have even offered me a job too, but I think I'd rather stay in my own line,' Maria went on.

'I'm sure you're right.'

'It's the reason why he went for those two days. He didn't want to raise my hopes earlier. Haven't I got the most wonderful man in the world?'

Trudi smiled at the enthusiasm in her sister's voice. She felt like telling her that Dan Johnson was the best man, but decided against it. She wanted to tell her sister that news when she saw her face to face.

'John and I have decided we might go to Bell Bay for our holidays next summer,' Maria continued. 'Tell me, did you see Dan Johnson again?'

'You might say that,' Trudi smiled.

'That's a strange noncommittal answer,' remarked

Maria. 'I think he quite liked you. Did you run away because of him?'

'No mere male would make me run,' said Trudi indignantly. 'Though I admit I think Dan Johnson is rather special.' She spoke quickly to distract her sister, having already said more than she had intended. 'I came back because we've got a chance of pulling off an Australian order. It could be a big deal.'

'I'm sure it will be fine,' said Maria confidently. 'What about coming down next weekend?'

'Sorry, if I'm not flat out I'd like to finish my holiday at Bell Bay. Possibly the week after?'

Maria's light laugh told her that her sister had guessed that Bell Bay held more attraction than sun, sea and sand. Hastily she finished the conversation and returned thoughtfully to the next task.

Unloading the car was speedily accomplished and she spread the tent out to dry at the back of the garage; Dan had told her that despite the heat of the summer the tent had absorbed quite a lot of moisture, and she recognised that he was right. By the time she had put everything away, she felt weary, but she made a cup of coffee and began studying the important notes. She was deep in the schedule when the telephone shattered her silence and she answered it mechanically.

'Trudi, I'm missing you already.'

Dan's voice spoke quietly, and immediately her papers slipped from her knee.

'Dan!' she exclaimed.

'You made a great hit with the Forrests,' he told her.

'Darling, you know I liked them. Anne's a lovely warm person and she'd gone to such a lot of trouble. They've got a great view from their lounge.'

'Not quite as good as from Ti Kouka,' Dan laughed.

'You and your cabbage trees!'

'Yours too, now,' he reminded her.

'Oh, Dan, I forgot to give you my present. It's only a bit of driftwood. I put it by my pile of firewood at the camp and it's probably still there. I hadn't finished it.'

'I'll collect it first thing tomorrow.'

'You'll recognise it,' she told him. 'I guess I'm getting as bad as you.'

'Mystery upon mystery! Darling, did you have a good trip home?'

'Perfect—I hardly noticed the distance. I wish it wasn't quite so far.'

'Never mind, honey. You are coming back to Ti Kouka this weekend? Official invitation!'

Trudi studied the comments Mr Maugh had put beside her papers. 'I'm not sure yet. Can I let you know?'

'Of course. I'd better let you get back to your papers!'

'Goodnight, Dan. I love you.'

'Goodnight, Trudi. I love you too.'

As she replaced the receiver she felt reluctant to renew her struggles with the papers, but determinedly set them in order before going to bed.

By the time the factory hooter started for work the following morning she had been at her desk for nearly an hour. She stopped briefly to say hello to Rita, but promised to catch up with the news later.

Briefly her thoughts went to Dan and she had a quick flash of him riding round the stock, perhaps gazing down at the campsite. Bell Bay would always be important to them, she knew. The page in front of her became a blur and she pulled herself back to the business in hand. When the buzzer calling her into Mr Maugh's office sounded, she felt quite ready to answer any of the questions the Australian might ask.

The meeting went well. The buyer set out a list of conditions and supply details. After he had left they were able to study them in greater depth. Both Mr Maugh and Trudi were surprised at the size of the possible order. She knew they could not cope with it. The profits were considerable. Trudi was glad the decision was not hers.

'Trudi, what have you dreamt up?' Mr Maugh wanted to know.

'I'm not sure yet. We could supply approximately three fifths by beginning two part-time shifts, or if we dropped a couple of smaller lines, or sub-contracted them.'

'Will you do some estimates now?'

'Yes—immediately.'

'Trudi, by the time you're forty, you'll be either a millionaire or a beggar!' grinned Mr Maugh.

Trudi smiled, suddenly thinking of Dan. 'Most probably the latter!' she acknowledged wryly.

After the boss had left she immersed herself in alternative schemes. All of them required detailed study and she was conscious of the clock striking eleven before she hastily put away her files and locked the office. When she arrived home she felt quite excited with the preliminary results of her efforts. The ringing of the phone made her think instantly of Dan.

'Sorry, darling, I've been working,' she apologised.

'Pull the other leg, Trudi. I've been sitting here going through agonies of jealousy imagining some smooth Aussie taking you out to dinner!'

'Nothing was farther from my mind or his. I've been flat out doing estimates,' Trudi assured him.

'I believe you, love. And you'll be tired, so I mustn't keep you. I just wanted to tell you I found the little cabbage tree, and it looks beaut. I'll give it to you in the weekend as I'd like you to finish it.'

'I'm glad you like it. Oh, Dan, I wish you were here!' Suddenly Trudi felt a pain of almost severe proportions as she wished Dan could be holding her and she realised how much she loved him.

'What time will you be up here in the weekend?' he asked.

'Dan, I'm sorry, I don't think I'll have enough time. We'll have to give some pretty firm figures and the deal we've been offered is so much larger that a complete analysis has to be done—and guess whose job that is?'

'Sweetheart, I guess I have to accept that.'

When she finally whispered, 'Goodnight,' Trudi replaced the receiver happily. Suddenly the world seemed full of wonderful enchantment. Even the figures she had been studying with such fascination a short time before seemed prosaic. She schooled herself to begin again and suddenly she noticed the work seemed easier as she could be more objective about the result. It shocked her to realise she would not be at the factory to see it.

She began her calculations, but found herself coming back to the same stumbling blocks. No matter which way she analysed it she knew they could not hope to meet the demand from their present site. She thought regretfully of the large building located next door.

On mulling it over she thought it was perfectly possible that the tenant, a signwriter, didn't need all the space he had been forced to take and would be willing to consider sub-leasing part of it. In the morning she decided to make the building next door her first call.

The young signwriter was already busy spraying a surface when Trudi walked in, and the odour of paint caused doubts. However, the man was waiting for her to speak.

Quickly she outlined her ideas.

'Miss Carr, you must be the latest in special messengers! Come in and look round—I'm wanting to leave as I've been offered a partnership in my first firm back in the North Island. I was committed to the lease here for five years and was thinking of approaching you folk.'

At lunchtime she contacted another friend, who was production manager at a rival company, and put out tentative feelers for machines. The grapevine had told her that the firm was switching the whole of its machining division to the North Island, so she was not surprised when her friend suggested they meet to discuss the proposition. After her meeting Trudi was pleased. She had been promised first refusal on the eight machines available, as well as additional equipment.

Just before work finished she presented her results to Mr Maugh. They began studying the details immediately, and on Mr Maugh's suggestion, sent out for a meal. It was almost eleven before they left the factory and Trudi wondered if Dan would still ring her. She hadn't meant to be so late, but the chance to finish the work uninterrupted had been a familiar compulsion.

Disappointingly, the phone did not ring and she found herself at one o'clock still waiting for it to peal. At three she had begun to feel sleepy.

To her horror it was almost ten o'clock when she woke.

Apart from a quick question about the benefits of sleep Mr Maugh astonished her by saying she must be in love. The telltale colour inking her cheeks had told their own story. Mr Maugh patted her hand and told her he hoped to meet the young man soon.

'Don't go rushing to get married, will you, lass? If I do decide on the new wing, I want you to promise to organise it and run it for at least a month so that the teething problems can be sorted out.'

'Mr Maugh, I wouldn't dream of running out in the middle of setting up,' she assured him.

'I know you wouldn't, Trudi. You've always been loyal and capable. Seriously, if you did leave I couldn't replace you. Rita's not accounts-orientated. We should give it some thought.' He put his cup down. 'I'm busy with the new sketches for Australia this weekend, Trudi, and I haven't had a chance to check the latest machine room figures. Could you go over them? There's the analysis of the output from the material too.'

Trudi hid her disappointment. There would be no chance to go to Ti Kouka. That night she explained to Dan, and his own disappointment made her feel a little guilty. When he suggested instead that he might call on Sunday, she was delighted.

Despite her doubts she dressed in her prettiest on Sunday just in case. The peal of the bell had sounded as she forlornly prepared a lonely salad for lunch. Trudi flew to the door and gazed unbelievingly at the large man who stood there. Her joyous cry of welcome was echoed by Dan's own greeting as he picked her up and held her close, before his lips met hers.

'I couldn't let another day go past without seeing you, darling,' Dan whispered. 'It's been the longest few days of my life. Every time I went to the camp I found myself thinking of you.'

'Especially when you were throwing the rubbish around?' teased Trudi.

'Especially then,' Dan nodded solemnly, only the

sparkle in his eyes giving him away.

He moved round the flat looking like a caged bear, dwarfing the proportions of the room, but his face turned down at her lack of outlook.

'A tin fence,' he smiled, and traced round the corner of her eyes.

'I know, Ti Kouka can show me a view for miles!' Trudi agreed.

'The faster I can get you to Ti Kouka the better. Trudi, you'll love it.'

'I love you, I don't care about Ti Kouka!' muttered Trudi.

'That's coming close to being a dangerous statement. Come up next weekend and you'll change your mind.'

'About loving you?' she teased, her hand on his chest.

She received the answer she deserved as Dan's mouth touched hers and their bodies met. The room seemed to explode into a dozen parts as she felt the lean hard muscles against her own softness. Her hands slipped around him as she felt his touch, very sure and gentle, she knew his own need matched her own.

'Trudi, when are we getting married? Let's surprise everyone and make it in a few days!' He kissed her again and Trudi felt her mind sway to his, then remembered her promise to Mr Maugh.

'Dan, we hardly know each other! We must be sensible. Besides, I promised Mr Maugh.'

'What on earth has your boss got to do with it?' Dan's eyes looked at her suddenly. Trudi reached up and curled her fingers through his hair and lay back in his arms, and the chill disappeared from his eyes.

'Dan, it's just that I promised I'd help with the new wing, if we go ahead with the export order. I've been doing a feasibility study on it for Mr Maugh. It would take a lot of effort if it goes ahead. It will be about nine or ten weeks, possibly more, if there are any delays.'

Dan looked at her with a mock groan. 'Woman, how could you agree?'

'Well, of course, he might decide not to go ahead with the plan, in which case I could leave in a few days.'

'You know what I'm hoping already, don't you? This is one export order I could wish elsewhere.'

Dan's voice was low as he kissed the small spot under her ear. His fingers found hers and he looked at her ring finger thoughtfully.

'Do you like emeralds, Trudi?' he asked. 'Mum has a ring she's been keeping for me—an emerald in the centre with two diamonds. It belonged to my great-grandmother.'

'It sounds lovely, Dan,' she agreed.

'You just say if you'd rather have a modern ring. I'm not quite broke!'

'Oh, Dan! Of course I'd be happy with your family ring. I've always loved emeralds.'

'That reminds me, Mum is very anxious to meet you. She said to tell you she's looking forward to welcoming you to Ti Kouka.'

Dan's voice dropped a little as he wound a curl round his finger. 'The tyrant's livid, of course, that she was away when you were at Bell Bay. Poor Anne's been pumped, but I assure you she gave a charming report.'

'Dan, what if your mother doesn't like me? What if the tyrant thinks I'm totally unsuitable? It would be dreadful!'

Dan laughed. 'That won't happen, don't worry. When will you know if the factory plan is going ahead?'

'Tomorrow.'

'Ring me immediately you know. If it's no, I'll drive down straight away and pick you up. Once you've met Mum and the rest you'll relax, then perhaps we could get married on Saturday.'

'Anne said you didn't let the grass grow under your feet, Dan!' Trudi laughed.

'Plenty of other places for it to grow on Ti Kouka.' Dan smiled and kissed her again, and Trudi thought she had never been so happy in her life.

'Dan, let's not hurry it so quickly. I feel it could be a mistake to rush in, we've got our families to consider. Let's leave it two weeks.'

They both smiled, then Dan's mouth claimed hers again and she slipped her fingers around the back of his neck.

By the time Dan left the night was well advanced and Trudi went off to bed humming a love song, wondering what it would be like to be married to him.

Going in to work the next morning, Trudi tried to immerse herself in the work in front of her, but at last pushed it away, gazing unblinkingly ahead as she saw Dan in her mind's eye, waiting for the telephone to ring. She felt oddly close to him and could almost feel his physical presence, his fingers holding hers for luck. She took one of the cups of tea that were just being poured and began talking to Rita, explaining that Dan had been down, when her buzzer sounded and she scurried into Mr Maugh's office.

'I've taken the lease,' he announced. 'Truth to tell, I really only decided this morning. You'll be glad?'

'Of course. I'll get started right away, but I've got a phone call to make first.'

Back in her own office, Trudi dialled Dan's number

and the phone bleeped only once before it was answered. She told Dan the news and he sounded so disappointed she forgot her own feelings. She reminded him that three months would soon pass and they could get to know each other better.

Just before lunchtime Mr Maugh called the staff together and told them of the proposed plans and called for further suggestions. He asked Trudi to explain and she was kept busy answering questions and discussing the changes.

Everything seemed to be roaring ahead almost as if the whole job was top priority, and Trudi was beginning to revise her schedule. She kept her fingers crossed for the weekend and told Dan she hoped to be with him by late Saturday afternoon, as the machines were being delivered in the morning.

'That's great, darling. We've got a big dinner party on with some overseas cropping experts, so you'll be arriving in good company,' he told her.

His words made her frown as she envisaged the scene. 'Dan, I don't think that's a good idea. You'll be tied up. I'll ask Mr Maugh to give me a couple of days off midweek instead and come up then.'

'Make it three days and I'll agree.'

'Dan, I love you, but you'll get me fired!'

'Do you mean that?'

With a smile she replaced the receiver. It was disappointing as she had worked hard to be free. Trudi imagined the scene at Ti Kouka. Dan, although such a junior employee, would be needed. He was so good with people, she thought proudly. Unfortunately if she was there he would look after her, and that could lead to trouble.

It would be just dreadful if the tyrant disliked her simply because she was a nuisance at an important time, and from such a nickname it sounded highly possible. Her smile slipped as she realised the difficulties involved in taking time off the following week. Tuesday and Wednesday were fully taken up with the new season's range. She wished there was someone who could step into her shoes. When Mr Maugh came in she discussed it with him. He suggested she study the new personnel files, adding that the grapevine had been well and truly busy as they had had thirty applicants for work, without even advertising.

Trudi felt glad, and reviewed the personnel in the factory, looking for the right person. Her eyes lit upon the neatly stacked application forms filled out in a myriad letters. On impulse she reached for them, thinking it a shame that so many would be disappointed. The second neatly typed form hit her with a sharp shock. She looked at it carefully and knew she had her replacement. She wrote 'Accept, Forewoman New Wing' across it, then dialled the applicant's phone number. The phone was answered by her friend, and hearing her voice Trudi chided her for not approaching her directly for a job. Her answer was that she had not liked to place Trudi in a difficult position.

'I feel so bad, as I approached you about the sewing machines and took it for granted you'd be transferring North too,' said Trudi.

'No, I thought about it, but with all the family here I didn't really want to move.'

'How does forewoman of the new wing sound? Come over after tea tonight and we'll have a chat.'

'Sounds great! Trudi, you're a gem.'

Smugly Trudy set off home. She felt as if she had just been given a million dollars. Finding her own replacement had been the biggest piece of luck imaginable. Best of all she could place her and then let Mr

Maugh 'find' her himself.

Her friend had asked about her young sister, as she had always enjoyed Maria's company. With a stab of guilt Trudi realised that the anniversary was almost upon her and she had forgotten that Maria would be eagerly expecting the pale blue outfit. It was just as well she was not going to Ti Kouka after all, she mused.

On Saturday morning she rang Mr Maugh and told him she wanted to buy some pale blue fabric for Maria's anniversary present. With a laugh he gave her the number and shelf card and told her to help herself. Trudi smiled.

'I'm coming in myself in ten minutes, so I'll cut it for you,' he commented.

Trudi had time to open up the storeroom and select the fabric before Mr Maugh arrived. She explained the design and he cut it out for her on the big designer's area.

'I suppose you're going to sit down and sew this now?' he queried.

Trudi nodded and Mr Maugh smiled.

'Let's see it when you're finished, would you, Trudi?'

'I'll bring it round this evening,' Trudi promised, then made her way to the silent machine room.

When the dress was finished she slipped it on. She wondered what Dan would think about it. Trudi had never worn draped effects, preferring simple styles. She pirouetted in a swirl of blue, seeing her reflection looking almost unbelievably pretty with her dark hair and her big eyes sparkling.

Thinking back, she couldn't remember Dan commenting much about what she was wearing, except for the memorable occasion she had danced on the beach in her silky green nightwear and he had called her a nereid. She could smile now at the fright and terror she had felt at seeing the enormous black figure rising from the water.

Surveying herself again, she decided that when she had some spare time she would make a slightly similar garment for herself, but in the sea-green colour that reminded her of the emerald waters of Seal Bay.

Mr Maugh had left earlier, so she dialled his number and he invited her to share dinner with him. Trudi agreed without hesitation; they would talk shop and it would be a beautiful dinner as Mr Maugh always appreciated good cooking. Dan wouldn't ring as he would be busy with Ti Kouka's guests.

Trudi drove around to Mr Maugh's house, the new dress carefully placed in tissue in a box beside her. She wore a simple dinner dress in brown with a beaded neckline which she had always liked.

On Mr Maugh's instructions she paraded the new blue dress with the right accessories and was rewarded with his approval. Although the brown was sophisticated and elegant, the blue seemed softer and more romantic. Mr Maugh declared it was a winner and suggested they include a similar style in the new range.

The hotel he had selected was one of the best and Trudi enjoyed herself, reflecting that this was a slice of life she would never see with Dan.

She found herself telling Mr Maugh about Ti Kouka and Dan and the day's V.I.P.s at the farm. Mr Maugh had heard of Ti Kouka and was vastly interested in her description. Immediately he realised the loss of her previous weekend and told her blithely that she could take off any time. When she reminded him a shade tartly that Tuesday and Wednesday were the range days he nodded.

'Thursday and Friday—the place won't fall to ruin without you, although I'll be screaming! I've got a present for you, Trudi, that I've been meaning to give you for quite a while—another bonus, my dear. That Australian order was all your work and now the new wing is coming along in leaps and bounds. There must be a lot of extra time in it. I'll see it's put in your pay next week.'

'Giving me Thursday and Friday off is all the reward I'd need,' she assured him. 'If you must give me a present I'd like enough of the sea-green colour in the fabric I made up for Maria today.'

'I'll make sure of it.'

It was quite late when Trudi drove home.

The doorbell woke her and she sighed, peering from her nest of blankets with surprise. The peal of the bell sounded again and she reflected that it was probably her cheerful but improvident neighbour, a young person who seemed to have trouble with household supplies. She grabbed her dressing gown and ran to the door, stifling a yawn. The figure who stood there had her smiling immediately.

'Dan! What a super surprise!'

'Good morning, sleepyhead. You look all soft and warm.'

He closed the door carefully and she melted in his embrace. His lips were gentle and questing and she felt her own response spinning.

'I'm jealous, sweetheart,' he murmured. 'I tried ringing you last night, but you were out. I went through sheer torture.'

'I was out at dinner. We had oysters creamed and flounder poached in wine and tournedos and. . . .'

'Stop, stop, my woman! You'll drive me crazy. Who

took you?' Dan's arms held her stiffly.

'Oh, Dan, you're jealous!' she chuckled. 'I was with Mr Maugh, my boss. In between all the food we discussed the current work and the new programme. Actually we got a lot of ground covered. And I told him all about you and he said you must be special to have found me!'

'Guess I'll believe you, darling. I was so disappointed when you didn't want to come to Ti Kouka yesterday that I started imagining all sorts of things. I'm afraid the guests must have found me a little absentminded.'

'I was sewing a dress for Maria at the factory,' she told him. 'Actually Mr Maugh came in and helped me with the design, and it's really pretty. Maria will be pleased. I thought I might make myself one, you might like to see me in a dress.'

'Make a change from nightwear and jeans and shorts, darling, but I think you're beautiful all the time,' he smiled slowly, and Trudi felt her own eyes light up as he traced the lines of a tousled curl on her forehead. 'Get dressed and I'll take you to the town house with me,' he told her. 'I've got to pick up some papers that were left there.'

'Will Mrs Jay be there?' queried Trudi anxiously.

'No, she's at Ti Kouka. Does that worry you?'

Her eyes met his and she shook her head.

'You know, love, I think you're a little coward.' Dan's words mocked her as she fled to her room. She showered and changed in speedy fashion after telling Dan to help himself in the kitchen. A glance at her watch had told her he had been driving since early that morning. She pulled on a casual shirt and jersey and skirt, easing on her boots and a leather jacket.

Dan eyed her warmly and she went to him and felt

his deep love wrap around her as he kissed her with a passion that made her sag against him, breathless. She left her hand in his as she stepped towards the car. Trudi had never studied cars very much, but she knew that this was not the average run-of-the-mill car.

Its engine barely sounded as they drove smoothly along the quiet streets and she knew from the superb interior that it was a luxury car. Sheridan Jay obviously allowed Dan the use of a car when he was on a Ti Kouka errand.

They drove up to Cashmere and soon Dan turned down a tree-lined drive. He swung the wheel and they faced a large garage which adjoined the edge of a new town house. Trudi was impressed. Obviously the 'tyrant' knew a superb setting.

The house was in gold brick with deep brown trim and the matching windows in aluminium blended perfectly. Dan flicked the key out with its distinctive holder and selected another key. Smiling, he opened the door, then picked Trudi up effortlessly and carried her over the threshold. She lay contentedly in his arms as he kissed her swiftly, then dropped her none too gently on to a deeply cushioned couch. She struggled to sit up as he peeled the thick curtains back from the window and revealed the richness of the furniture. Trudi hastily moved her booted feet.

The lounge was quite one of the loveliest rooms she had ever been in. On the plain back wall a bush picture caught her eye and she found herself entranced. She gazed at it and turned to Dan who was standing watching her.

'It's beautiful,' she said. 'Your tyrant must be a remarkable woman.'

'I'd agree with you there.' Dan sat beside her and

pulled her close, and she lost herself in his arms for a few blissful moments.

Dan stood up slowly. 'I won't be long. I've just got to get those papers. Make yourself at home.'

He went off beyond a doorway and Trudi stood at the window looking out at the view over the city below. She could pick out the familiar lines of the city centre and the angles of streets. A whistle distracted her and she noticed Dan standing at the doors that evidently opened off a verandah. She ran along to see him, and her breath drew in as she gazed into the room. It was luxuriously appointed and Dan was sprawled on the bed as though he owned it.

'Dan!' Her tones were full of reproach.

'Sorry. Was I a bit long?' he enquired innocently. 'Come on in, sweetheart, and help me sort through these papers.'

Trudi hung back. It was all very well for Dan, but it didn't seem right for her. The magnificent old carved desk that was in the bedroom had been an heirloom, a glance revealed that. She shook her head at Dan's easy nonchalance.

She almost ran back to the lounge and her eyes were caught again by the painting on the wall. Frowning, she went up to it, then stepped back as though stung. The work was an original.

'Do you like it, Trudi?' asked Dan. 'I bought it for the tyrant a few years ago. Rather good, isn't it?' He held the papers he had obviously been sent to fetch.

Weakly Trudi nodded. The thought of Dan buying and giving away a work of art shouldn't have surprised her, she guessed. At least the 'tyrant' had appreciated the gift as it was in pride of place. If only Dan had kept the painting himself it could now be used as a down-payment on a house, she thought soberly.

'What are you thinking about, sweetheart?' he queried.

'Must be my sordid nature, Dan, money! I guess that painting would be worth a great deal today.'

'Yes, but only if you sold it, and it won't be sold. It's a gift, not an investment, darling.'

Trudi studied Dan thoughtfully. She realised that he never seemed to care about money, and she could only marvel. She supposed Mr Jay must have seen that he always had enough for his needs and living at the farmhouse his board would be included in his wages. If everything was supplied at Ti Kouka she supposed it was possible that Dan had never grown conscious of money. It seemed strange to her, but her own struggles had made her too conscious of its lack. She let Dan take her in his arms and felt the warm touch of his mouth drive out all thoughts.

'You are the most incredible man,' she whispered. 'I love you, Dan Johnson.'

'Much more and I won't guarantee good behaviour, woman!' he murmured as he kissed her.

As she waved goodbye to Dan later, Trudi felt supremely happy. Her world was complete with Dan. There would be all sorts of snags ahead, but with Dan life held an extra promise. A man who could give away a painting and only rejoice in the owner's good fortune when it turned out to be so valuable was a special person indeed.

Her whole world had been turned upside down by the man from Ti Kouka. She grinned, thinking of the little tree which she had whittled so happily. One day soon she would finish it.

A familiar car pulled up outside the flat and she greeted her mother happily. She made her mother a drink and told her about Dan. Her mother smiled and told her daughter that happiness was shining out like a beacon on a black night.

'Your father would have been pleased to see his two girls so happy. I know I am. Bring Dan over soon.'

'Mother, no wonder Dad loved you!' Trudi bent and kissed her mother, and after she left she realised that now she could see her own mother's new happiness too.

CHAPTER SEVEN

ON Wednesday afternoon, after the sample range had been viewed, the atmosphere in Mr Maugh's office was one of mutual congratulation. The meeting had gone extremely well. All the garments selected were carrying their new numbers.

'Before you go home, Trudi, what about having dinner with me tonight? By the way, did you like your pay slip?' Mr Maugh sounded pleased.

Trudi smiled. 'You won't believe it, I know, but I haven't even glimpsed it. It's probably still sitting on my desk! I'd love to have dinner with you so long as I'm home early, as Dan might ring.'

'Fine, I'll ring and book an early meal. I feel after the view today we've got quite a lot to celebrate. I'm going home now. I'll pick you up at six-thirty.'

Trudi smiled and agreed. The figures looked very good and the enthusiastic response to the new designs from the reps had reassured them. Small wonder Mr Maugh was happy! She made her way back to her office and saw the pay slip envelope on the desk. She opened it, then sat back into her chair with a small disbelieving squeak. She studied it again, shaking her head in disbelief. The amount she had been given was the equivalent of three months' wages. It explained why Mr Maugh had looked so smug when he asked if she had seen her pay slip. Hastily she dialled his number, but the uninterrupted buzz told her he was not yet home. She could hardly wait to tell Dan, knowing he would be delighted. She grinned, thinking that they could have a honeymoon after all. Although Dan had told her jokingly that he was not quite broke, she guessed he had little saved for such an event, certainly he had never mentioned it.

She decided to dress up for the evening. She would have little chance with Dan. A glance at the large old clock on the office wall told her she would have to hurry if she wanted to put her hair up.

As she wound her hair into a series of shining curls she glanced at the telephone, wondering if she should ring Dan before she went out. She had expected him to ring during the day, but then realised that his call had probably not been put through as she had been in conference so much of the time. Promising herself she would return home by nine, she finished her dressing and promptly at six-thirty saw Mr Maugh's familiar car swoop into the park outside.

As he came towards her Trudi walked forward and kissed him on the cheek, thanking him warmly for the cheque. He patted her arm, reminding her it was well deserved. The hotel was busy and Mr Maugh mentioned that an Agricultural Promotion Conference was being held there. Seeing the outdoor men around her reminded her immediately of Dan, but she smiled at the thought of his ever being in such a position.

The service was considerably slower, but they had plenty to discuss. They were still discussing work when a glance at her watch told Trudi it was half past nine. A burst of laughter from behind her made her wish she could see the cause of merriment at the tables that were being used by the farmers' groups.

'Did you see in tonight's paper that your boy-friend's boss is one of the new members of the promotion board?' Mr Maugh asked her.

'Sheridan Jay?'

'Yes, he was born with a golden spoon, not a silver one.'

'Pity I didn't fall in love with him,' grinned Trudi. 'At least no one will be able to say I'm marrying Dan for his money. He hasn't a bean.'

'Well, I'll give you a good wedding present, lass. Sounds as if money might be the answer.'

'Mr Maugh, today's bonus is quite enough,' answered Trudi firmly. 'Dan will be pleased, and if he can be torn away from Ti Kouka long enough, we'll probably have our honeymoon on the strength of it.'

'Doesn't sound like my sensible, practical Production Manager at all!' Mr Maugh shook his head. 'Are you wise to rush into this marriage, Trudi? After all, you hardly know the fellow.'

'Once you've met Dan, you won't worry,' Trudi stated. 'I'm going to Ti Kouka tomorrow, so I'll meet his boss then, I dare say. I'm more worried about meeting the boss's mother. They call her the "tyrant" among themselves.'

'Don't you fret, Trudi. You've nothing to worry about.' He patted her hand in a fatherly gesture. 'Worry about the placement of the new lights instead. Come to think of it, I remember my wife designed a special bracket and stand years ago. I've still got the designs at home.'

'That could be helpful,' put in Trudi.

'I'll look them up on the way. We can have coffee there. It would take another hour here, the service is slow tonight.'

Trudi agreed, then glanced at her watch surreptitiously. Mr Maugh, being so methodical, would be able to locate the plans within a few minutes; she could make coffee in that time and still be at home at least by ten-thirty. She waited patiently as Mr Maugh signed the chit. A large group of farmers walked down the corridor and she stared, thinking one was Dan. She shook herself, knowing it must have been some other tall dark-haired man in the soft lighting of the hotel.

She slipped into the big car and sat calmly, trying not to see her watch and the precious minutes ticking away. It would have been lovely to have said 'Please drop me at home, I'll see the papers next week', but she knew she could not be so churlish. Another quarter of an hour would not be too long, she thought, before she could ring Dan and explain.

As they pulled up at the large ornamental gates and the car nosed its familiar way Trudi couldn't help a fleeting envy at the thought of the large empty house. Stepping into the lushly carpeted foyer, Mr Maugh switched on lights and the warmth of the heated rooms welcomed her.

'Make the coffee, Trudi, and I'll run upstairs and see if I can find those papers. If I can't find them immediately I'll give you a call.'

Trudi nodded and went off to the kitchen. It suddenly hit her that Rita and Mr Maugh would make a good match, and she wondered why she had never thought of it before. Both were nice people, both had seen their lives altered tragically and both had matured through it. Mr Maugh was shy of strange female companionship and Rita had spent her efforts concentrating on her family. Smiling at the thought, she decided that in the coming weeks she would do her best to see that Rita and the boss were thrown together. If Rita was to do Sales and Publicity, she would take the former advertising office next door to Mr Maugh. The thought had all sorts of possibilities, Trudi realised, as the coffee hissed and bubbled. She watched the tiny

stream of pale liquid gradually darken, then prepared
a tray. As she was entering the lounge Mr Maugh came
down the stairs holding the papers. They studied them
as they drank the coffee.

Trudi could see the value of the design and they
soon became involved in a discussion. The soft chiming
of a clock made her look at the time with a frown, and
Mr Maugh gathered up the papers.

'I must run you home, don't want you missing your
beauty sleep for the all-important meeting tomorrow.
Goodness, the time has run on!'

Mr Maugh escorted her to the flat and she bent forward and kissed him quickly on the cheek as she
opened the door. He said goodnight and then went
back to his car.

The precious papers she put down on the lounge
table. Dan would not ring now, she realised, instinctively glancing at the phone. She must have been
at Mr Maugh's place for an hour at least. She unclip-
ped her hair and it fell in fat curls around her face,
making her eyes large and deep. She pulled a face at
her reflection and turned away thoughtfully to pick up
her purse with the cheque safely tucked inside. She
smoothed it out, studying the design of the paper
absently. The peal of the doorbell shocked her out of
her reverie, and she wondered at its almost urgent
sound. She put the cheque on to the table and opened
the door.

'Dan, what a surprise!' she exclaimed.

'Surprise? You didn't expect me tonight, obviously.'

The street light emphasised the dark lines of his face,
so that he looked like the ancient Rangitira, pride,
anger and vengeance at war in his stance. He slammed
the door behind him and the sharp bang made Trudi
wince in alarm.

'Dan, whatever's the matter?'

'Don't try and act the innocent, Trudi. You really have been keeping me on a string, haven't you? What's the matter? Been trying to work out which way you can have your cake and eat it too?'

Dan's eyes lit on the cheque on the table. He picked it up and eyed it incredulously.

'Well, at least he pays well for your time. Money—that's all you care about! I hope it satisfies you. I must have been mad!'

'I don't understand, Dan.' White-faced, Trudi stood looking at him.

'Come off it! Trudi, I saw you at the hotel—there was a dinner I had to go to. You told me you couldn't spare a minute today or yesterday because of work. I tried to ring you several times and you were always out, or in conference. But tonight I saw you dining with an old man, and you had plenty of time for him. You gave him all your attention. I had to stay put, but I could watch you. When our party broke up at the same time I thought there could well be some simple explanation, so I followed you, intending to surprise you.' Dan's eyes glittered, his face harsh. 'I saw the lights go on upstairs and that tubby little guy starting to undress before he realised the curtains weren't pulled.'

'Dan, stop it! You're wrong! Mr Maugh isn't like that—he's just my boss.'

'So what does it matter who he is, so long as he has money?' The scorn in Dan's voice cracked icily. 'I remember now—you said you were thinking of marrying him. He's old enough to be your father!'

Trudi sank back on to the sofa shaking her head in stunned disbelief, as she tried to explain.

'No, Dan. I made some coffee and we had a couple

of liqueurs, then went over some business papers to-gether. You must be. . . .'

'Mad? Yes, I was crazy about you.' His mouth twisted into a straight line. 'You played me like some tantalising fish. All the time you couldn't come to Ti Kouka because of work!' He paced the floor, then snapped to a stop in front of her, his voice bitter. 'Oh yes, it was work all right, but it certainly wasn't any-thing to do with the factory, only the boss!' His eyes raked her, hard and chilled. 'You have such an air of innocence, yet so much sensuous appeal. Well, now it's my turn.'

He reached for her and pulled her towards him in a grip of steel. His mouth descended, silencing her pro-test in a hard, angry movement. This time there was no trace of love or gentleness, only a blinding, searing rage. Trudi struggled against the iron body inef-fectually, feeling the scrape of the dinner jacket he wore bite into her tender skin. Tears formed in her eyes and she put all her strength into pushing Dan away, and some of her terror must have penetrated as he stopped to look at her.

'Dan, no!' Agonised, she looked at him.

'Don't worry, I don't like second-hand goods,' he spat, and released her. He thrust her back on to the sofa, her body limp as a rag doll. The slam of the door told her that he had left, his anger still raging. Tears spurted down her face, muffled by the velvet of the cushion. Her lips were tender and she put her fingers to them as though to shield them from further ill usage.

The whole scene flashed before her and she groaned in misery. She stifled a sob, wondering about Dan's comments, her brain beginning to function again as she pieced the evening together. She remembered the boss telling her that Sheridan Jay had been voted into membership of the prestigious committee. He must have taken Dan along to enjoy the success, as the dinner had been an all-male affair. Dan must have spotted her, but he could hardly have joined her in the middle of speeches or during dinner, she reasoned.

If only he could have sat close enough to have heard their innocent conversation about work, she thought sadly. She frowned, recalling that Dan had said something about Mr Maugh getting undressed. It didn't make sense to her—till with a gasp she realised that Mr Maugh had changed his shirt while he was upstairs. Over dinner he had complained of a prickling sensation at the back of his collar of his new shirt. She could even remember laughing about it, suggesting that he had left the pin from the packaging in the cloth. Thinking about it, she knew that Dan had seen Mr Maugh pull off his shirt. Probably only then had Mr Maugh drawn the curtains. She could visualise only too well Dan's stunned imagination. If they had not taken so long over coffee the situation would have righted itself, but the time had sped and to Dan every second would have been like an hour. The agony and anger on Dan's face when he saw the cheque flashed before her again. She couldn't blame him, the build-up of evidence had been totally crushing. The cheque had been the coup de grâce. Trudi gulped back the tears which kept rising in her throat.

It was ironic, she thought, that Dan should think she was so money-hungry, when she had agreed to marry him. She went slowly to the bedroom and her mind flicked her a vision of herself in Dan's arms when she had coolly announced that she might marry her boss. It had been totally ridiculous, of course, and she had known it immediately. To Dan, it had all been part of the same picture. But he now believed that she had been having a long-standing relationship with Mr Maugh. Her desire to get back to work, her inability to get to Ti Kouka, all fitted. Each day she had been able to tell Dan little of the exciting work she was handling as she had never discussed her boss's affairs with anyone. Tiredly she undressed, and crawled into bed.

'It would never have worked, Trudi,' she told herself. 'You've been your own boss for so long, you couldn't have married a man like Dan.'

This instruction to herself had the disastrous effect of filling her eyes again, and she burrowed her head in the pillow, letting the misery she felt completely overwhelm her.

The morning was well advanced when she woke feeling heavy and miserable. Her eyes were still puffy and ringed with red and she wondered if she had cried even in her sleep. Her lips felt oddly tender and her finger touched them gingerly. It was just as well she was not going in to work today or there would be a few raised eyebrows. She felt ill and turned reluctantly to the wall. In her mind's eye she pictured Dan at the creek, seeing the laughing sense of challenge he had issued and his rich amusement. Then she saw him at the rock, talking quietly and gently, treating her as delicately as a piece of sea foam.

She wondered miserably what Dan would have said at Ti Kouka that morning. It would be embarrassing for him to have to admit that she would not be visiting. Dan would not give any explanation, she knew instinctively.

Shuddering, Trudi got up; she had to keep busy, had to drive the thought of Dan away.

As she showered, the cold showers at Bell Bay

crossed her mind, but the self-inflicted thoughts of Dan only made her more miserable than before. When she had dressed she began spring-cleaning the flat in an orgy of work, to banish the dark angry eyes and the firm well sculptured mouth she knew so well.

The cheque and the papers lying on the table she carefully put away. The cheque had cost her dearly and she bitterly regretted encouraging Mr Maugh to find the old papers. If she had only insisted on leaving them till her return, she told herself sadly. Dan would not have been so jealous; he would have understood. She could have explained about her bonus and the completion of the decisions on the range. Her shoulders drooped as she thought of Dan, riding the horse towards the beach, his mouth a hard line, as unyielding as the rocks, standing as a guard before the sea. He would never return to her.

She scrubbed madly at the windows, rubbing the spots viciously in her despair. They glinted brightly at her, reminding her of the diamond sparkle on the waves at Ti Kouka. She finished the task, then made herself a drink, forcing herself to concentrate on pouring the water into the coffee. She remembered the trek Maria had to get water at Bell Bay, and how Dan had approached her, his eyes chill over the drink bottle at the top of the ridge. Now she had seen all the feeling whipped from him, so that his eyes had been frozen, and she rubbed her eyes to stem the tears.

'Do something, girl. Go somewhere. Somewhere Dan's image won't follow.'

She walked up to the local shop and bought some groceries, carrying the heavy load back mechanically. Back at the flat again she looked around with fresh eyes. The flat was tidy and the interior that she and Maria had refurnished neatly and wallpapered brightly, but the lack of outlook suddenly appalled her.

Compared with open vistas for hundreds of miles at Ti Kouka, the neighbour's fence was an affront. Trudi felt shut in, trapped by the four walls that had been her home for so long.

Picking up her keys and her purse, she slammed the door behind her, then climbed into her car. Stooping to fasten the seat belt with mechanical movements, she eased the car out. The drive took her towards the south and she kept along that route thinking that every mile took her further from him. Long before, he would have returned to Ti Kouka. Perhaps he had stayed at the flat belonging to the Jays last evening, or perhaps he had driven back to the farm then. She creased her brows, hoping he had returned safely.

Her route stretched open before her and she kept the car heading south, glad that she was being forced to concentrate on the road. The mountains stood in the far west and for a minute she felt tempted to turn, but then the thought of Maria stopped her, and she decided to keep heading south until she reached Ashburton. The car petrol gauge was showing almost full as everything had been checked carefully the day before in readiness for her trip to Ti Kouka.

Maria would be delighted at the surprise visit. Trudi wondered if her sister would be at home. Driving at least stopped her thinking of Dan. If Maria was out she would ring John at work and he would be able to tell her whether it was sensible to wait.

Having a destination gave her something to think about and as Maria knew almost nothing of her relationship with Dan, she would not be expected to say anything. Although Maria was not the type to say, 'I told you so', she thought wryly. The brown grasslands

of the plains reminded her that Dan had said most of
the country was feeling the lack of rain. In the city she
was barely conscious of the weather, considering only
how the next section of the new plant was going ahead
and whether the builders would return again. An oc-
casional crop of wheat or barley showed golden but
served to emphasise the dark dryness of the usually
fertile soil. Evidently the countryside here had not
received the rain the week before.

It was a relief to reach the outskirts of Ashburton
with its attractive trees lining the edges of the road.
She drove into the town and stopped at a fruit shop to
purchase strawberries and raspberries. At their old
home she had grown her own and Maria had loved
them. She bought some other small luxuries, knowing
they would be appreciated.

As she pulled up outside the modern block of three
flats, Trudi felt glad she had come. At least the awful
depression of spirit she had felt had lifted slightly at
the thought of seeing Maria. Guiltily she realised that
her sister had so little time left in Ashburton and
once she was in Wellington, it would be a much more
expensive or lengthy trip to see her. The front door
was open and she called out her sister's name tentatively, seeing the stacks of boxes in the middle of
the floor.

'Trudi! What on earth are you doing here?'

There was surprise and pleasure in her sister's voice
and Trudi looked admiringly at her. Maria had had
her hair cut even shorter and seeing Trudi's glance she
twirled.

'Like it? I just had it cut this morning, ready for the
big city life again. I'll put the jug on. Sit down, if you
can find a space somewhere! I've just been packing
some gear. John's friend is taking an empty car up to

Wellington in a couple of days, so you've caught me in an awful muddle.'

'Sorry, I should have rung, but to be honest, I didn't know I was coming,' Trudi explained.

'That doesn't sound like you?'

Too late Trudi realised that Maria's sharp mind had quickly sensed the oddity of her words. Typically, Maria said little, after a quick glance, and Trudi realised shamefacedly that she was wearing a cotton skirt and blouse so she could not pretend to be on a work expedition in such casual clothes.

She put the baskets on to the kitchen bench, stepping carefully around the mounds of tissue paper and clothing. As Maria was busy putting down cups in the small dining area she asked about the latest news, and her sister gleefully told her that her former boss had contacted his friend, a lawyer in Wellington, and she had been offered an interview for the day after they arrived.

'I'm thrilled, because he's a first-class court man,' she explained, her eyes sparkling. 'And his office is just round the corner from John's firm! We're both so excited about it. We'd thought of coming up to see you this weekend, but you're always so busy, Trudi.'

'I know. We've got this big push going at work and I've been involved in setting up a new extension. After the next couple of weeks things should steady slightly. At least we'll be operating then, so I won't be needed in twenty places at once.'

'You work far too hard, Trudi. You look simply dreadful, big bags under your eyes, and if you were any slimmer each breeze would bowl you over!'

'Thanks for the vote of confidence, little sis!' said Trudi dryly.

'Honestly, Trudi, it's time someone said something to you. I've tried ringing you until all sorts of hours and never any reply. You know I had to ring the factory to get through to you last week.'

'Don't sound so cross, please, Maria. I have been working hard, but from next week I'll be a reformed character. And I mustn't let you run down Mr Maugh—he's given me a huge bonus.'

'So I should hope!' snorted Maria.

'So don't say he doesn't appreciate my efforts. Besides, it's been wonderful having a more or less free hand to work things the way I want them.'

'I hope this bonus doesn't mean you've got to work harder?' said Mania.

'Maria! No. It was simply Mr Maugh's way of saying thank you.'

'O.K., I'll simmer down and say the man has his generous side, certainly,' smiled Maria. 'Oh, Trudi, you are a poppet to bring me strawberries—and raspberries too. Lovely!'

'I won't have you so near to spoil soon,' sighed Trudi. 'Still, you'll be able to fly down easily enough.'

'I'm thinking I should consider learning to fly. It would be less costly.'

'That's a thought. Maybe when I have some time I could take it up myself.'

'Yes, and we could land at Bell Bay and have super times there. I'm sure Ti Kouka has its own airstrip,' Maria added innocently. She saw her sister's face whiten and stopped to ask gently, 'What's the matter, love?'

'Nothing, now,' answered Trudi bleakly. 'I loved Dan, and it didn't work out—end of story.'

'Trudi, I'm sorry.' Maria hugged her sister sympathetically, then her eyes softened. 'I told you he was a gorgeous man. Don't worry, Trudi, he's the type to appreciate an independent mind. It'll come right, you've probably had some minor sort of row and the world looks as if it's falling apart, but something will happen and the situation will right itself.'

'Regretfully, this was a bit more than a minor tiff,' Trudi said wearily with an attempt at a smile. 'It's finished. Please let's forget it, Maria.'

Maria was about to say something, but obviously thought better of it, seeing Trudi's white face and haunted expression. Instead she began to talk about Wellington and the expected changes it would mean.

When John arrived home their love and comradeship made Trudi realise again how much she had lost, and it was almost a relief to leave. On her way home after dinner the thought of the happiness she might have had with Dan almost overwhelmed her. She was glad the road was deserted and when she arrived back in Christchurch her flat seemed unbelievably empty. The years of being a career girl seemed to stretch ahead without meaning. The little tree she had carved so happily at Ti Kouka tormented her, and she picked it up before hiding it tenderly in a drawer.

In the morning she wished she could go back to work, but she felt unable to face the thought of the inevitable questions her presence would raise. The sight of the lighting adaptation on the table made her seize the plans gladly. She could at least do a feasibility test there.

She made a few notes and contacted the firm who handled most of the engineering for Maugh's Fashions. The boss agreed to see her immediately and she went off to discuss the papers with him. So long as she kept occupied her mind didn't revert to the disturbing picture of that shattering last scene with Dan.

When Monday arrived she dressed herself as carefully as possible and set out for her office. It seemed a snug shelter from the stormy winds, and only Mr Maugh's smile as he asked her how her stay went shattered her. For a moment she wondered what to say, realising that if Mr Maugh knew how his actions had been so misinterpreted he would be upset. At last she just said that Dan and she had agreed not to see each other again. She felt Mr Maugh's sympathetic touch on her shoulder and was glad when he quietly left. Rita must have been told, as she didn't come charging in full of enthusiasm as was her normal style, but instead suggested that Trudi visit her for tea. Trudi accepted gladly, thinking that playing Monopoly with Rita's family would keep her occupied for another couple of hours.

Maria and John had to visit Christchurch the following day and she had arranged to throw a small family dinner party. Studying her own reflection, Trudi could only conclude that she could do a passable imitation of the witch of Condor. Her make-up hid some of the ravages.

Acting lighthearted was one of the hardest things she had ever done, but she managed it, and towards the end of the dinner she had almost convinced herself that it was just as well the whole affair was finished.

Waving Maria and John off later in the week from the airport, she hid her desolation, assuring Maria that she really had got over the 'hunk' astonishingly quickly. Somehow she managed to produce a mirthful comment about summer romances, not withstanding the chill of autumn. The airport *would* have cabbage trees in the car park, she thought bitterly, as she unlocked her car. The sea of hurt came rolling down once her sister's plane had turned skywards.

At work the new wing was nearing completion and the

machinists were busy on the next styles. Doing the thousand and one routine chores appealed, demanding her concentration. It was almost as if Mr Maugh and Rita had decided to close ranks to keep her more occupied than ever. The night before the new wing was opened Mr Maugh suggested they have a celebratory dinner. Remembering her earlier idea of matchmaking between Mr Maugh and Rita, Trudi suggested that as Rita had done such a lot of the work, she should be invited too. The dinner automatically reminded her sharply of the last occasion with Dan, but the happiness on Rita's face and Mr Maugh's made her wonder if her scheme had a chance of success.

For once everybody was early the next morning. Mr Maugh performed the introductions and then flicked the power switch on in the new wing, to good wishes and cheers. The familiar song of the machines sent everyone scurrying, and Trudi watched for a moment as the new section began to hum with activity. The new lights worked well, she noted automatically. After watching and assisting for a little while she could feel the room settle as the staff found their routine. She walked thoughtfully back to her own office and closed the door. For so long she had worked for this moment, yet now she knew only a sense of anticlimax. Work seemed empty and meaningless.

At lunchtime the bell sounded early and she went reluctantly along to the staff canteen. She knew Mr Maugh was throwing a lunch party for the staff and she knew she had to attend. To her surprise her entry was greeted by applause. Mr Maugh made a speech and presented her with the first garment. To cries of 'Model it!' Trudi retired to try it on, knowing she had to satisfy everyone.

Back in her office she opened the box, and the colour of the sea at Ti Kouka swirled as she pulled it out. With pain she dressed, automatically noting the soft glamour of the gown. She combed up her hair and redid her make-up quickly, then walked in to more cheers. A press flashlight dazzled her temporarily and she posed obediently as the reporter asked her for details of her career. Evidently Mr Maugh had explained about the success of her efforts for the Australian order and the new wing. Changing back to her business suit again, she was quite touched by the gesture in giving her the gown. She doubted if she would wear it again; it was too feminine, too romantic, too much a dress for a girl in love.

CHAPTER EIGHT

THE morning paper landed with a soft thump on the drive in to the flats, and Trudi slipped out of bed to get it. Absently she split the band covering the paper, then climbed back into the warmth of her bed. The paper fell open and her gaze was riveted on the large picture of herself under the caption 'Dollar-Earning Doll'. The small print beside it explained that she had been instrumental in obtaining a large export order for Maugh's Fashions and in order to fulfil the order the company had opened a new wing, creating valuable jobs. The article went on to detail a few aspects of the company and another photo showed Mr Maugh and Rita standing by one of the new machines. Trudi read it through hastily and then studied her own picture. She had to admit the photographer had taken a good shot. Rita would be pleased with the publicity the company had received. Her lips twisted as she pictured Dan's reaction. He would be sure to see it and would probably agree that the caption was more appropriate than the paper had known. She could imagine him crushing it in his large strong hands and throwing it into the fire.

The whirr of the alarm startled her, so vivid was the scene she had drawn for herself. Walking to work, she became aware of the cooler weather, the summer which had been so brilliant was losing some of its warmth. At Ti Kouka the waves would be crashing in full force on to the sand and the Rangitira would be covered with each spray. Trudi shivered suddenly and was almost glad that the image of Dan standing staring out to sea was broken by Rita's call.

'Isn't it a beauty! You look fabulous, Trudi!'

'You're not so bad yourself,' countered Trudi, 'and even the boss looks quite smug. I wonder if it was only the new wing he was smiling about.'

Rita blushed. 'Alf's a dear. It's amazing how you can work in the same building for so long and never know a person. I'm not saying anything will come of it, but it's rather nice to be taken care of and to be cherished when you've been on your own for so long. I'd forgotten,' she ended with characteristic simplicity.

'I'm delighted,' Trudi smiled.

Trudi turned into her own office with a grin. That revealing 'Alf' for Mr Maugh had given her a real clue. When the mail was brought in she studied one Australian letter closely. The prospect of another order was pleasing.

It seemed as if Trudi could not put a foot wrong as the next two weeks went past. The orders turned out from the new wing were almost exactly as she had anticipated and her friend was proving a godsend. Trudi appreciated the easing of her workload and commented on it to Mr Maugh at their weekly meeting to review progress.

'What about taking some more of your holidays? They were interrupted, and Rita still scolds me about that.'

'I would like a week off just to relax, but later on I'd like longer, to stay with Maria and John,' said Trudi.

'You fix it up, just the way you like.'

A letter from Maria, ecstatic about her new job and the challenge it offered, reassured her. Maria's and John's happiness seemed to glow, as the descriptions of house-hunting and their excitement at finding a home of their own flowed from the letter. Trudi felt the pain gnaw at her again as she remembered that if she had married Dan they would never have had a home of their own.

A vision of Ti Kouka's homestead swung into view as she remembered her first glimpse of it sitting in the sun. Dan's face came back to her and she knew that living at Ti Kouka, even if it was crowded with others, would be wonderful if only Dan had been there with her. Dave and Anne Forrest had the ideal answer.

The peep of the telephone broke up the painful thoughts.

'Trudi, it's the first time I've come down to pick up the boys at school, so I thought I'd ring you and say "hello".'

'Anne, you won't believe this, but I was just thinking of Dave and you and Ti Kouka. How lovely of you to ring!'

'Come and visit,' invited Anne, 'I'm staying over-night at the flat.'

'Anne, I'd love to see you, provided it wouldn't embarrass anyone. Dan isn't there, is he?'

'Dan? No, the men are miles away at a conference in Wellington. Mrs Johnson isn't expected back till after the movies. She's gone to see the latest science fiction with an old friend, so you've no worries. I would like you to come.'

Trudi felt her heart racing at the thought of hearing a little more about Dan. Surely it wasn't stupid to want to know that he was all right?

'I'll come, about seven-thirty,' she said.

'Lovely! You remember the way?'

'Yes,' Trudi said softly. She could remember so many details of the visit she had made there with Dan.

She replaced the receiver after a quiet goodbye, then felt the tears begin to form at the back of her eyes. Anne Forrest would have known her romance was over. It was nice of Anne to still want her friendship.

Promptly at seven-thirty Trudi slipped into her car. She had taken considerable pains with her make-up and her dress was one of her prettiest. Anne would be sure to notice such details.

'Trudi, I'm so pleased you could come!' smiled Anne.

Trudi was ushered into the familiar room. Her heart pounded again as she saw the picture of the forest which Dan had given Mrs Jay. Rapidly she glanced back to Anne.

'How are the boys and Dave?'

'They're fine. The boys are back at school, so the usual routine is settling. We were so busy last month. The harvest is over for another year, thank goodness. The men worked like oiled machines, dawn to dusk continuously.' Anne paused reflectively, as she took Trudi's jacket. 'I was sorely tempted to tell Sheridan Jay to get cooled off in the sea. Really, he's been impossible lately! Even the tyrant got her head bitten off when she tried to reason with him.'

Trudi smiled weakly. 'Poor Dan,' she commented sadly, thinking that as he lived in the same house life would have been uncomfortable. She could not resist asking any longer, 'Tell me about Dan, is he very unhappy?'

Anne shook her head. 'I'm not sure that's the word. Dave and I were so pleased when we saw you together. He just reminded me of a big glass of champagne fizzing and popping with the joy of living. Now, he's still the same, but all the sparkle has gone—as though someone had left the champagne to go flat, stale and sour. You don't have to tell me about it,' she added hastily. 'I'd hate you to think I was prying. I just wondered if there was anything we could do. You see, we love him too.'

Trudi looked down at the floral pattern on her skirt. She realised that the dainty spray was an artistic clump of pink, red and white starry manuka flowers. Subconsciously she must have associated it with Bell Bay and Dan.

'I don't think anyone can help. I love Dan and I guess I always will, but the whole situation is a disaster. Let's talk of something else,' she ended desperately.

'I'm sorry, Trudi. I guess while Dan's been going through agony, you have been too. You're looking very pale, you need a bit of fresh air. Trudi, I've just thought,' Anne added. 'Why not come home with us for the weekend? I'll be returning on Sunday night to drop the lads back at school. I'm picking them up at nine o'clock in the morning, so transport's no problem.'

'I'll think about it,' said Trudi uncertainly. She longed to say yes. It would be heaven to wander along the cliffs, to hear the sound of the bellbirds and the tuis again, and to scramble over the rocks in Seal Bay. Every memory of the magical time she had spent with Dan came to her mind. If Dan was away she would not be hurting him.

'Please come. I know you loved Bell Bay, everyone does. The boys are longing to get home. Whether they think differently when they're older Dave and I sometimes wonder. Since the experimental wheat crop tests the boys have become quite research-minded. The crop figures we achieved this year were highly significant. The Council of Wheat Control has invited the boss to give a breakdown on the latest figures at the conference.'

'We didn't get round to talking much about the growth of wheat,' Trudi smiled.

'I don't suppose you talked much about the factory! Dave and I saw your picture in the paper the other day. You looked fabulous.'

'I was lucky.' Trudi paused. 'I didn't care for the caption, I'm afraid.'

'That was the one thing my son commented was appropriate.' The voice was cool but dignified. Trudi looked up in surprise. The softness of the carpet had hidden the entry of a tall, dark-haired woman whose elegance was completely natural.

'Mrs Johnson, I'd like you to meet Trudi Carr,' said Anne. 'Trudi, this is Dan's mother.'

Anne's quick words fell into the silence as Trudi and Dan's mother looked at each other. The intelligent brown eyes reminded Trudi of Dan at once. In fact, the arctic frost in them made her think of that time when Dan had made her feel small about the forgotten bottle. She could feel the blood draining from her face.

'I'm pleased to have the chance to meet you for myself,' said the older woman. 'Unfortunately you were too busy to accept my son's invitation to visit us at Ti Kouka.' The frost disappeared by magic as she turned to Anne. 'It was a wonderful movie, incredible special effects! My friend's granddaughter wanted to come with us, so we decided to go to the five o'clock session. Are you a fan of science fiction, Miss Carr?'

Trudi could only admire Mrs Johnson's social sense. Evidently she did not wish to embarrass Anne Forrest.

'Some I've seen I've enjoyed. I don't go to the movies much, somehow there's never seemed time.' She knew her answer was ragged.

'Work is your great interest, I understand. I know the label, of course. As a matter of fact I have three of your gowns in my wardrobe this minute. Tell me about that export order you achieved.'

Faced with such a royal command Trudi explained briefly, minimising her efforts. Mrs Johnson's shrewd questions showed a knowledge of the trade and Trudi found herself relaxing as she explained in greater detail.

'I'm sorry, I was talking too much,' she apologised.

'Nonsense, it sounds fascinating.'

For the first time Trudi felt the warmth and sweetness of Mrs Johnson's smile. Instinctively she smiled back, unable to resist.

'I'll make a drink,' put in Anne, suiting action to words by getting up and moving to the kitchen.

'Thank you, Anne.' Mrs Johnson glanced at her again and Trudi felt the older woman's sadness. 'I can see how much your career must have meant to you. I'm not blaming you now I've talked to you. I was before, I'll admit.'

'I would have given up my career for Dan,' put in Trudi slowly. She felt she had to be honest with Mrs Johnson. 'I've discovered just how inadequate work is now. Although I've been so busy, the second I stop, I see Dan. I can't seem to avoid thinking about him.'

'I think Dan is doing the same thing. We've always been very close, but over this I can't help him.'

'I'm sorry, Mrs Johnson. All I can say is that Dan misunderstood something. He's not to blame—I am.' Trudi's voice had tailed into silence. 'It's funny really.'

'Except that you feel like weeping instead of laughing?' put in Mrs Johnson, patting her arm gently. 'The only clue I've got is that laugh when my son saw the picture in the paper. I don't ever want to hear such an ugly, tormented sound again. I believe he thinks you're a gold-digger.'

'And worse,' Trudi sighed, her eyes studying the carpet thickness without even taking it in. 'Please, Mrs Johnson, it's no use. I'll always love Dan, but I know there's no future in it. I'm glad I've met you, because you'll help him in time. I'm glad he has such good friends as the Forrests, and his boss must be pretty good too.'

'His boss?'

The conversation was getting almost beyond Trudi. She hoped desperately that she could avoid the tears that were gathering at the back of her eyes and throat.

'Yes, the wonderful high and mighty Sheridan Jay of Ti Kouka. As for Mrs Jay, the sound of her scares me stiff!'

Anne walked in with a lavish trolley and Trudi was glad to select one of the many featherweight delicacies Anne had prepared.

'Anne, you're a gem!' Mrs Johnson smiled. 'Miss Carr was telling me the thought of meeting the Jay family was intimidating. Do you think the boss of Ti Kouka is very fierce?' Her voice had an attractive lilt now and its echo again reminded Trudi of the humour in Dan's.

'Well, I'd hate to get on the wrong side of him. But I doubt whether it would ever happen.' Anne's eyes smiled widely. 'But of course, as for the tyrant, words fail me!' Anne's eyes lit with laughter, and Mrs Johnson chuckled.

'Forgive me, Trudi. Be assured that the tyrant isn't as bad as she sounds.'

'She must be quite nice, because Dan thinks the world of her,' contributed Trudi.

Anne coughed into her handkerchief and Mrs Johnson smiled widely.

'Tell me, Miss Carr, what position do you think Dan holds at Ti Kouka?'

Trudi reassured her hostesses. 'I'm under no illusions, at all. I know Dan is just the hobo around the place. It's funny, but all my ideas went topsy-turvy when I fell for Dan. He's just such an unworldly guy and I guess I was too materialistic! I really hated the thought of never having our own little place. Now I've had time to find out it wouldn't matter if I lived in a tent with Dan. Just being with him would make it fun.' She shrugged her shoulders wistfully. 'I'm sounding like a bad soap opera!' She was glad that neither of the two women moved. She supposed her comments must have sounded dreadful.

'My dear, I'm going to call you Trudi—really I can't go on calling you Miss Carr. I think if you came to Ti Kouka you'd find it a lot easier to understand. Come home with us in the morning.'

'I'm sorry, I would love to see the homestead, but I wouldn't wish to embarrass Dan,' protested Trudi.

'If you come with me tomorrow Dan won't even be there. Everyone's away. It really is a golden opportunity,' added Mrs Johnson thoughtfully.

'Anne had already asked me, as a matter of fact,' put in Trudi honestly.

'Trudi, we'd love to have you, but I'll withdraw my invitation for another time. Quite frankly, I think you must go to Ti Kouka.'

'Do come, Trudi,' begged Mrs Johnson, 'I hate being on my own at Ti Kouka! It's such a large house it needs people. We're driving home early and Anne can bring you back to town on Sunday evening. It would be kind of you to give me some of your time.'

'I can see where Dan gets his charm from,' capitulated Trudi. 'I'd love to see Ti Kouka, Dan spoke about it so much.'

'I must send that little one a book or some sweeties. If I'd gone to the eight o'clock session I'd have missed meeting you,' put in Mrs Johnson with a smile.

As she drove home shortly afterwards Trudi thought Mrs Johnson's remark was typical of the graciousness of Dan's mother. It had been a surprise to meet her, yet she seemed to contribute even more to the puzzle. No one could overlook Mrs Johnson easily. She had a completely natural air and warmth, yet her first glance had almost frozen Trudi.

Anne Forrest and she obviously thought the world of each other and she could imagine Mrs Johnson being a cross between a grandma and an elder sister to the Forrest family. It was strange that such a striking woman could live in perfect peace with the 'tyrant' of Ti Kouka. The 'tyrant' wouldn't be able to persuade Mrs Johnson to do anything she didn't want to. Smiling at that thought, she climbed into bed and allowed herself to daydream. Supposing things could be explained with Dan, suppose she were to meet him again, suppose his arms would enclose her and she would feel the heavens wheel as his mouth touched hers.

'Stop daydreaming, Trudi,' she reminded herself sternly. 'You've got one weekend to gather memories.'

In her dreams Dan held her tenderly and whispered that he loved her. It was hard to wake up to reality. She showered and washed her hair at the same time, then dressed neatly. By the time her gear was packed she just had time to eat a hasty breakfast before the arrival of Mrs Johnson. She locked up the flat and stepped into the car, recognising the late model car as being a saloon model of the type Dan had driven. Again the small cabbage tree design dangled from the key ring, but this time the centre of the tree had been decorated with greenstone. Sitting quietly in the back with the boys, Trudi found her eyes travelling to it. Evidently Mr Jay supplied a household car too, she thought.

The turn-off to Ti Kouka seemed to come slowly and when the shingle road was finally reached, with its distinctive cabbage trees, she could re-echo Mrs Johnson's profoundly simple statement, 'Home!'

Trudi looked out the window. The creek where they had first met Dan flashed past and then soon afterwards the car slowed as Mrs Johnson eased off the accelerator, just as the car rounded the corner to reveal the first view of Ti Kouka homestead. Trudi drew a sharp breath, looking at the scene she had pictured so many times. This time there was no horseman riding along the track.

Her thoughts were broken as the boys announced they had arrived at the bungalow. Their joy could hardly be contained as they burst out of the car the second it stopped in front of their house. Trudi waved goodbye to Anne with a faint misgiving, feeling suddenly apprehensive. Mrs Johnson turned the car and headed towards Ti Kouka. The homestead gates were open and as they drove towards the slight rise Trudi moistened her lips.

One day Dan would hear that she had visited them, but she hoped by then the pain of their last meeting would be over.

'My dear, welcome to Ti Kouka,' smiled Mrs Johnson.

Past the huge macrocarpa trees and the clumps of oaks, then at last Ti Kouka sprawled itself lazily in the sunshine. The two-story old stone dwelling had darkened to a dull grey, but the house was redeemed from being too dark by the enormous windows. Two small columns supported a large porch which Mrs Johnson drove under so that they were immediately outside the front door.

'I'm giving you the full treatment, Trudi, front door entrance.'

Mrs Johnson seemed completely at home as she opened the door with the key on the chain. Trudi found herself in a large reception area and a magnificent old grandfather clock ticked softly. A faint whirr startled her as it began to chime. The deep melodious sound reminded her instantly of her childhood home and she felt welcomed by the sound.

'It belonged to the original Sheridan,' smiled Mrs Johnson, 'or rather to his bride Mary.' She led Trudi into a large sitting room and Trudi stopped to admire it. A well proportioned spacious room, with its crystal chandelier sparkling in the sunlight, showed the magnificently plastered ceiling. Comfortable rolled arm couches and matching chairs were grouped attractively. A grand piano stood in one corner, but it scarcely obtruded. At the far end a large stone fireplace occupied the greater part of the wall. A distinctly homely atmosphere was in the room, despite its size.

'Through here is the dining room and off that is the breakfast room,' commented Mrs Johnson. Trudi followed wide-eyed as she glimpsed a period Victorian dining suite complete with ornate buffet. The chairs around the table seemed sufficient to feed three families.

'I'll show you round in a minute, but first let's put the kettle on. Oh, by the way, that end door in the hall goes down to the shepherd's wing; we never go "visiting" unless invited. It keeps everyone's dignity.'

'So they have their own rooms?' queried Trudi.

'Yes, it's really an apartment. They have a bedroom, a guest room, a lounge, and of course a kitchen and bathroom. It was modified years ago. My flat is the same, immediately above theirs.'

Trudi nodded. She guessed Mrs Johnson was accustomed to running Ti Kouka. It would be a large task, the standard was immaculate, so the tyrant must be a demanding mistress. Mrs Johnson led the way, pointing out the downstairs bathroom and toilet facilities, the television room, the games room and then Sheridan's study. They went back to the hall where the stairs led a curving way up.

'What a wonderful staircase for a dramatic entrance,' Trudi commented.

'You're absolutely right. I've really enjoyed it on many occasions. Here we are, you have this room. I'm sure you'll like it.'

To Trudi's surprise she was in one of the central bedrooms. It appeared almost overwhelmingly grand. She lowered her bag as Mrs Johnson told her to make herself comfortable, before joining her for a cup of tea. After Mrs Johnson had disappeared Trudi surveyed the room. The bed with its heavily carved head and foot boards was matched by the dressing table and tallboy. Two comfortable chairs stood in a corner as though gossiping with each other about the newcomer. The curtains were brightly patterned, highly glazed cottons, which matched the coverlet on the bed. Large windows led her to look out at the view. She could glimpse the red roofs of the Forrests' bungalow in one corner of the patchwork of rich fields.

A horse grazed in a paddock close at hand, and she recognised it immediately as Dan's. She turned back to explore her room. A side door opened into a dressing room with drawer and wardrobe space fitted round three sides and mirrors along one wall. She grinned as she hung her lonely dress and jeans in the august space provided. A similar space was on the opposite wall. Another door led into a bathroom and she stared in astonishment. The floor area was in proportion to the house. The room had a large shower cabinet in one corner, which despite its impressive door handle was glisteningly modern, matching the other facilities.

Another door led out of it and feeling a little like Alice, she followed where the door led and found herself in another vast bedroom. She stopped immediately feeling herself an intruder. A faint familiar tang made her wrinkle her nose and she smiled as she recognised Dan's aftershave. Instinctively she gazed around with delight, knowing she was in Dan's room. A large sitting area was formed by the porch which led to the front door immediately below.

A view all over Ti Kouka spread before her, because of the three aspects of the window. She stepped to one of them and admired the neat paddocks, then turning, she could see the sea in the distance. Her fingers picked up the binoculars on the ledge and she jumped suddenly as the tall cabbage trees on Ti Kouka Point appeared. Her fingers automatically felt a small plaque at the side and she put them down, seeing the inscription, 'To Dan—love, the Tyrant'.

Three photos hung in a row on one wall and she moved forward to study them. The first was a sight that made her smile. It was a charming study of a man, a woman and a small boy. She had no difficulty in recognising the small boy as Dan, and Mrs Johnson had not altered greatly. She guessed the lean spare man was Dan's father. The next was a more casual study of the same man talking to Dave Forrest. His bronzed countenance showed delight in some joke shared with the photographer, and Trudi wondered if Dan had been the cameraman.

Below it a sepia portrait of an elderly stern-faced unsmiling couple caught her gaze. She knew instinctively she was looking at a picture of Dan's grandparents. The man, though elderly, had a toughness about him, a grim determination that contrasted oddly with the gentle grip of his wife's hand. He glared out at Trudi fiercely and she stepped back, feeling guilty.

She fled back through the massive bathroom and dressing room and then stopped. A man's jacket hung on the opposite wall and she gazed at it, recognising it immediately. Sliding back the door, she saw that the wardrobe on that side was almost full. Dan's suits and trousers and shirts hung neatly along. Thoughtfully she shut the cupboard and returned to her bedroom.

She guessed the house could hold more surprises as she made her way downstairs.

'Let's use the breakfast room,' suggested Mrs Johnson. 'It's beautiful with the sun at the moment. The tea is just ready to pour.'

Trudi smiled at her hostess. 'Sorry, I went wandering. I ended up in Dan's room.'

'Don't look so guilty, child. The rooms do connect, after all. The whole suite was changed a couple of years ago.'

'Dan told me the homestead was as big as a barn, but I had no idea. I thought everyone would be living on top of each other, but it's not like that at all. I guess I was wrong about a lot of things,' Trudi said, perplexed. 'Why doesn't Sheridan Jay have the master suite?' She blushed, realising her curiosity had made her sound discourteous.

'He does,' put in her hostess with a sympathetic smile. 'There's such a simple explanation, you know. Would it help if I told you that Dan is short for Sheridan and J is the initial for Johnson?' At Trudi's startled gasp she smiled. 'The name Sheridan James Silas Turnbull Johnson is rather a mouthful! Initials were so much easier, they just stuck. His father was James and he was very keen on calling our son Sheridan after the old man, so I insisted on putting in Turnbull for my father. We both decided that as the rest of the initials matched his pioneering grandfather's, he'd better have Silas as well. Some call him Dan, others S.J.'

'So my Dan Johnson is the high and mighty Sheridan himself?' breathed Trudi.

'Indeed,' laughed Dan's mother. 'Though I'm not so sure about the high and mighty title!'

'And you certainly are no tyrant,' added Trudi, recovering her surprise. 'Thank you for telling me. I've been so stupid! It makes so much sense I wonder I didn't see it before.'

'The obvious does! Just think what the first man to use the wheel must have thought. Another cup of tea?'

Drinking the hot fluid, Trudi felt slightly foolish not to have discovered the truth before. It seemed as if she didn't know Dan at all. Mrs Johnson took her arm gently.

'Don't be upset—it's understandable, and it's proved a valuable point. I know you're no gold-digger, Trudi. You told me you'd be prepared to live in a tent with Dan! His father and I knew that Sheridan would be a target for gold-diggers. Regrettably several girls have made their interest in Dan's money patently clear, and Dan developed a rather cynical attitude, but I hoped that one day he would meet a girl who would love him for himself.' Mrs Johnson broke off and collected the dishes and automatically Trudi helped her to carry them out to the gleaming kitchen.

'I'll pack you a picnic lunch and you can go wandering if you like,' her hostess said kindly.

'I would appreciate that,' put in Trudi gratefully. 'I don't know how you were ever called "the tyrant"!'

'Thank you, Trudi.' Mrs Johnson chuckled. 'As a matter of fact my father called me by the name one day when I was throwing a tantrum at the age of two. I was so shocked I stopped my performance immediately! I'd always been an indulged youngster, but my parents knew that there were limits! When I met James, my father passed on the information and it became a family joke.'

'No wonder Dan spoke so fondly of the tyrant!' exclaimed Trudi.

'Poor Trudi! It's a shame that Sheridan wasn't here this weekend. We could have sat down and discussed it all—I'm certain we could have cleared up a lot of misunderstandings.'

Trudi shook her head. Deep within her she knew that Dan would be too angry to sit calmly and listen to her side. There were too many misunderstandings.

Mrs Johnson handed her a cut lunch and waved her goodbye. Trudi set out, her heart full. She heard the swing door clang behind her and it seemed like some mocking echo.

In a surprisingly little time she had reached the sea and she turned towards the rock where she had perched so long before. The approach to the rock was a little slippery and she cautiously scrambled up to shelter on top. A seagull's cry mocked her, and she turned and retraced her steps.

As she walked along the sand she headed towards

Bell Bay. She munched one of the sandwiches, grateful
for her own appetite. Gradually the beach opened out
as it formed the gentle curve, before turning to form
the small beach and meet the sheer white limestone
cliffs.

Bell Bay was deserted, only a few sheep contentedly
grazing where their tent had been pitched. They scat-
tered as Trudi approached and she sat on the plank
Maria had positioned. The pile of stones that had
formed their fireplace still held burnt ash and she
poked it absently with a stick she had picked up. The
ashes had been dead a long time, she realised. Like the
ashes of the fire, Dan would never rekindle the flame
of love which had drawn them together. Despondently
she made her way back, even as a bellbird began to
sing.

She was glad to reach the homestead, conscious of
her own weariness. There had been so many moments
of pain as she tramped over the beach at Bell Bay, but
the most shattering moment of the day had been when
Dan's mother had told her Dan was S.J.

CHAPTER NINE

THE morning dawned cloudy but mild and Trudi, dressed in her jeans, shirt and sweater, ran down to the kitchen. After breakfast she did the flowers, then Mrs Johnson handed her a back-pack loaded with a picnic.

'Off you go, get some fresh air. Will you go over to Bell Bay again?'

'I'd like to go to Seal Bay.'

'It's magnificent, but dangerous on your own. You could go with the Forrest boys; they know the area.'

'It's all right, Mrs Johnson. There are plenty of other beautiful places.'

'I've packed extra in case you see the children,' said Mrs Johnson.

As she set out Trudi found herself accompanied by small dark shadows, and turned to see Dan's two dogs, the sleek black and white huntaways. She fondled them, feeling oddly glad about their patronage. Recognised as official party, they scampered around her eagerly as she made her way to the high point. Gazing around the panorama, she could understand so much of Dan's love for the land. She ate some of the food, then rested against the rustling cabbage trees. From her viewpoint she saw the three younger Forrest children and ran lightly down the track to meet them. They expressed immediate eagerness to visit Seal Bay, and they all set off at full speed towards the white cliffs. Almost winded, Trudi was glad to slow to enquire as to the whereabouts of the eldest member of the family.

The laconic reply 'Homework!' reminded her of her own school schooldays.

'The dogs can go home now, they might bark at the seals,' piped little Robin.

With a final pat for the dogs the children followed as Glenn began scrambling over the rocks. Trudi realised there was a lot more water than there had seemed when she visited the Bay with Dan, but the steadiness of her young guide reassured her. She turned to assist Robin, who gave her a beatific smile, and jumped gleefully. Totally unprepared, Trudi felt herself slip as the child landed beside her. Even as she gripped the ledge a wave dashed against her and her arm and one side were soaked.

'It's O.K., just a bit of salt water!' Trudi laughed at Robin's aghast expression. 'Just preparing me for the rainbow spray; look, the sun's just peeped through the cloud.'

'It's like fairyland, isn't it?' breathed Robin.

'No seals! Let's hunt for crabs,' put in Glenn.

Trudi made her way to the log she had sat on earlier with Dan, stopping occasionally to pick up the odd shell.

'I think it's going to rain, the clouds look black,' put in Glenn later. 'The tide will have sealed over the rocks by four-thirty, so we have to get going soon. How's the time?'

'Only four o'clock,' checked Trudi.

'Not now, Glenn! Look, there are the seals!' little Robin's voice whispered excitedly.

'Sssh! They're coming in!' Her big sister Angela's eyes were large.

In rapt silence they watched the seal family. Trudi wondered if it could be the same group that she had watched with Dan. If so, the puppies seemed to have grown enormously since her last visit, their grey-brown bodies darker and the fur thicker.

The children smothered laughter as the little seal plopped cheekily against his mother and using her body as a springboard dived into the water. He repeated the process, his cheeky black eyes glistening.

'The seals are beautiful,' put in Angela dreamily.

They chuckled together, but Glenn looked at the water. 'I'm wondering if I misread the tide table, the sea looks heavy.'

It was an odd word for the boy to use, but studying the sea Trudi saw it was appropriate. It rolled quite differently from the manner in which it had crashed into the little bay when they first arrived. Frowning, she looked towards the gap and stood up anxiously.

'Glenn, I think we'd better get going. I'm no expert, but it seems to have come awfully close,' she said.

'That's the closest I've ever been to the seals,' said Robin ecstatically, as they climbed the rocks.

Her words didn't reassure Trudi. If the seals were close it could only mean the tide was farther in than they thought. She knew from Dan's words on their earlier visit that Seal Bay could entrap as the entire area was covered each full tide. The cliffs reared starkly beside them and she glanced at them, thinking they looked dangerous, pockmarked as they were with holes and pillars and caves. Busy in her thoughts, she stopped suddenly at the water in front of her. The stones were completely covered. Robin's cry of consternation made her bite hard on her own fear.

'Glenn, wasn't there a cliff path?' Vaguely she remembered Dan mentioning it. They quickly turned and Trudi helped Robin and Angela to jump down from the rocks and make their way back across the strip of sand. They began running, crossing to the far end where Trudi could see a darker cliff with scrubby bushes on odd ledges. It wasn't limestone, she noted with relief.

'We can't go that way,' Glenn exclaimed. His fingers pointed out the path. 'Last year with Dad you could see almost the whole way up. But there's been a slip.'

'At least we could go part way.'

Together they climbed on to the path's first ledge. Trudi knew that unless they could reach a cave above high water mark they were still in danger.

'I don't know anything about the caves. The boss and Dad would never let us go near them. I remember seeing one a bit higher up; there it is, behind that bush,' Glenn finished excitedly.

'Stay here and I'll have a look.'

Trudi scrambled up the track and shuddered as the path ended in a sudden drop. Already the sea spray splashed her, and she knew the time was slipping away. She turned and saw another ledge laden with logs and driftwood slightly higher. With a maximum of effort she reached it, then hauled herself higher again into the cave. With relief she found herself able to stand upright.

It was almost pitch dark in the cave and she had to force herself to wait until her eyes adjusted to the gloom. Gingerly she explored the area. It opened out rather like a large room and shelved down gradually at the back. At least it looked safe and was above the tide line, she thought with relief.

A hurried glance at the children waiting silently on the ledge made her sing out cheerfully,

'Hey, we've discovered a fantastic pirates' lair!'

She scrambled back down to them, marking her footholds carefully. Leaving Glenn with Robin, she carefully helped Angela into the safety of the cave.

Again she made her cautious way down to the widest gap and studied the distance. Inside herself she knew that the smallest child could not reach the last ledge.

'Glenn, you hop up and pass Angela some of the firewood from the lower ledge, but be careful.'

'Sure thing!'

With relief Trudi slid down to Robin, whose smile wobbled slightly.

'Robin, I think I'll just have a rest by you for a minute before I take you up.' She smiled to make light of the situation, then turned her eyes desperately to seek an alternative route.

'We need a bulldozer,' commented Robin.

Her words were an inspiration.

'Guess I'll be the 'dozer blade and you can be the 'dozer,' said Trudi. 'We have to stay joined until we reach the cave. That can be the garage, right?'

'O.K. Do I make the 'dozer noises?'

'All the best bulldozers do!'

They edged their way up to the closest point, a small ledge several feet below their objective. After a glance below, Trudi determined not to look down again. She signalled a stop and spoke to Glenn above her, before turning to Robin.

'This time you can be the blade and I'll be the tractor. You climb on my shoulders. I'll hold your feet and then Glenn can reach your hands, O.K.?'

'Sure! We'll make it.'

Robin's trust warmed her. The noise of the sea was very close, the spray reaching for them, but she would not look. The darkening sky made her frown and she looked at her watch, wondering how long they had been. It still stood at ten past four. She knew then what had happened. When her arm had been dunked some water must have seeped into the watch, gradually slowing it until it stopped.

'Off we go!'

Carefully pushing the child ahead of her, she reached for the last holds.

'I've got her!'

Trudi didn't dare sigh with relief until Robin entered the cave. The children were all babbling excitedly and Trudi pulled herself up, conscious that her side ached, her shoulders felt bruised and her hands were badly cut. She had never been through such a terrifying experience and she didn't dare to think of the downward journey. Temporarily the children were safe.

'Gee, I'm starving!'

'Me, too!'

'The pack—it's on the ledge! I'll get it in a minute. There's quite a lot of food left.'

'Will we have to stay here all night?' questioned Robin, her eyes wide so that for a moment she looked like her bigger sister.

'Course we will! Probably till lunchtime when the tide is low again. I don't think we could do that trip down the cliff in the dark. It would be different if Dad and Sheridan were at home, they'd soon have us out. I hope we get out before they get back, though. Dad's going to skin me alive.'

'Nonsense, it wasn't your fault, Glenn,' Trudi reassured him. 'I've just discovered my watch has stopped.'

'It's dark in here,' put in Robin. 'Can we light a fire?'

'Sorry, I've just realised I've no matches.'

'Here, but please don't tell Mum.' Glenn's shamefaced expression made her grin.

'Just what we wanted. Look after them and I'll see

if I can fetch the big log I noticed earlier, and the pack.' Trudi made her way down to the ledge. The sun had disappeared and the cool grey of the evening had the bite of the rain in it. Grabbing several logs and the pack, she made her way back. Not far from the cave stood a much bigger log and Glenn was tugging at it.

'It's matai, and it's dry,' he explained.

The two of them shifted it to the entrance, then studied their prize.

'If we could keep pushing it on to a fire at one end it would burn for hours,' Trudi said hopefully.

'Trudi, I'm cold!'

'Here, Robin, have my jacket. We'll soon have a fire going.'

They didn't need Dan Johnson to tell them what to do. Trudi remembered Dan telling her not to sit on the rocks as they were cold, so she pushed some of their precious logs into a small floor area and suggested they all sit together. With the fire lit the atmosphere took on a much more cheerful tinge.

'At least Mum will know where we are,' put in Angela. 'The smoke will tell her. It's rather fun, isn't it! Can we eat now?'

The picnic was never more appreciated.

'I'm sleepy, Trudi,' muttered Robin, nestling contentedly against her. 'Tell me a story.'

Trudi thought for a moment. The simple demand made her think of her own childhood. The sound of the sea reminded her of her father's story of the pearl, and Robin was fast asleep before the tale was finished.

Angela took the next turn and then Glenn had them shivering with a ghost story. Gradually Glenn and Angela settled, and Trudi reassured them, telling them that she would keep watch. The three children soon lay asleep and she covered them with her cardigan. The night would be long, but sleep had never been further away. The thought of Dan's anger was enough to keep her wide awake. Bitterly she wondered if she could leave Ti Kouka before Dan returned from the conference.

She shivered and rubbed her arms before adding another log. Her watch caught her eye and she noted that it showed four-fifteen. A small sharp twig lay at her feet and with it she prized the back off her watch. In the firelight she could glimpse the shiny workings. She held it out to the flame and rubbed the empty case with the cotton of her blouse. She doubted whether it would work, but she supposed the fire could dry it. Carefully she edged it together, setting the watch by guessing the time.

Looking at the length of the matai log, she wondered if she could locate a similar one by which they could clamber down the cliff the next day. She began to ponder on their situation. Without the danger of the tide she might be better to leave Glenn in charge and to go down on her own to get help from Ti Kouka. Considering the problem, she stood up again and made her way to the edge of the cave. The moon was a feeble sickle, which scarcely cast any light, but at least the clouds had rolled away.

Below, the sea leapt hungrily, but already the tide was ebbing, she realised. She remembered the dawn descent from her island with Dan.

A spark snapped suddenly, sounding like a gunshot, and Glenn sat up swiftly. His puzzled glance took in the surroundings, then he recollected himself.

'Is it my turn to watch?'

'I guess it is. What about us talking for a little while?'

'Fine. Look at these sleeping beauties. Honestly, it would take an earthquake to wake them!'

'Well, you can pray we don't have one of those,' grinned Trudi.

'Facing Mum and Dad will be bad enough. Poor old Mum, she'll be baking, I guess.'

'Baking?' Trudi queried.

'Sure, she reckons she thinks better when she's doing something. When we get home there'll be a feast waiting! Don't know if I'll be given much of a chance to sample it, though. I'll be in the dog box for a while.'

'Well, I'll be there too,' smiled Trudi. 'I'm worrying more about the way down.'

'Oh, no problem. The boss and Dad will have help on the way at first light.'

'They'll still be in Wellington,' Trudi reminded him.

'Oh, no. They were going to catch the late ferry and drive straight through. Guess they'll be arriving at Ti Kouka any time now. S.J.'s got all sorts of rescue gear in the store. He'll be here as soon as the tide's cleared the stones.'

Trudi's heart sank at his words.

'Are you certain the men will be catching the late ferry?'

The boy paused with a shade of doubt. 'Sheridan might decide to stay longer. Dad will be wanting to get back, though.'

Trudi clung on to the hope that only Dave Forrest would return that night. With luck she could still leave before Dan returned. She couldn't expect Mrs Johnson or Anne to drive her home, but there could be a bus.

'Do you ever catch the bus back to school?' she asked.

'Yes. We just grab it at the turn-off to Ti Kouka. It

gets there about nine in the morning, but it can come slightly earlier or later. It waits on the ferries and sometimes that causes a delay.'

'Do they stop for you?'

'Sure, no problem to wave them down.' Glenn stretched and pushed the log again, then pulled the jacket around him closer. Trudi saw him recognise it.

'You gave us the jersey and your jacket,' he commented. 'You're all right, I reckon.'

Oddly warmed by his words, Trudi crept to the entrance. It seemed darker than ever, and her heart sank. The wind still whistled and she thought at first that the sound she heard was a trick of the wind. When it was repeated she called Glenn, hastily explaining to him. The whistle sounded faintly again, and Glenn emitted a piercing whistle in turn.

'That's Dad's whistle. He's way over by Kiwi Hill!' Mum thought we were going there.' The boy's voice was excited and they listened carefully, holding their breaths, waiting for a response.

'Whistle again,' commanded Trudi. 'Try calling.'

'Wouldn't do any good if they can't pick up the whistle. However, I'll try again. Whistling carries, and the dogs could react even if Dad doesn't hear us.' Glenn emitted two more ear-shattering blasts. This time another whistle closer at hand sounded in immediate response, the pitch changing in mid-note.

'That's Sheridan! He's heard me. Hear him acknowledge?' The boy's pleasure was obvious despite the dark. Heart dropping, Trudi turned back, wishing she could blot the next few hours away.

She winced as Glenn's whistle sound shrilled again. The distinctive whistle replied immediately.

'Sheridan sounded closer. My guess is that he'll be driving the truck. I'd better give a blast every few minutes. He'd relay our position to Dad on the walkie-talkie. You listen, Trudi, I reckon we'll hear Dad in the jeep soon on the top ridge. He can cross country, whereas Sheridan will have to drive back to Ti Kouka and round.'

A revving of a motor shortly afterwards was followed by Dave Forrest's anxious voice calling from above them.

'Glenn?'

'Dad! I'm glad to hear you. Did you have a good trip?'

There was a strange-sounding snort, then Dave shouted again. 'Are Angela and Robin and Trudi with you?'

'Sure, Dad. We're in a big cave well above high water line ten feet west from the old path. We're fine.'

'O.K. I'll pass on the information to your mother.'

A brief silence followed and then Trudi heard the sound of another vehicle, and knew instinctively that Dan had arrived. A moment later she heard his voice speaking to Glenn. His tones sounded kindly enough as he explained that he had picked up Anne Forrest on his way. Even as she heard Anne's voice the children stirred. Glenn reassured his mother and then Glenn signalled to Trudi.

Obediently she told Anne that the children were in good shape, then heard Dan issuing an order. Dan's voice sounded crisp and cold as he told her that seeing they were safe temporarily it was advisable to wait until dawn. He informed her that they would be immediately above them should they need assistance.

Trudi walked disconsolately back to the fire, but even with throwing on all the wood she couldn't get warm. Chips of ice from Dan's voice seemed to have settled in her heart. Robin woke and began crying, and she comforted her quickly.

'The boss didn't sound very pleased,' volunteered Glenn. 'Guess I'll be in big trouble.' He sounded so worried that Trudi put her arm around him, assuring him it was just his imagination.

'He would have been a bit worried about you.'

'I suppose you're right. They haven't had any sleep, and it tends to get people scratchy, doesn't it?' He yawned and settled down again.

Trudi nodded. Her own lack of sleep had caught up with her. The sight of the fire dying down woke her instantly to alertness. Hastily she broke off a couple of the bark chips and twigs and, thus encouraged, it blazed again. Glenn had settled and within a few minutes his even breathing made her smile. He at least had trust in their imminent rescue, and wasn't too scared of the master of Ti Kouka.

She watched as the grey light crept over the sky. A scrabbling sound alerted her to someone's arrival. The light was blocked by a dark figure silhouetted against the opening. Instinctively she put out her hand to help.

'That's not necessary.' Dan's voice was cold, like the angry seas. 'This isn't the time or place to say what I want to say.' His eyes raked her like sharp knives before turning towards the sleeping children. 'Can all the children move? Any injuries?'

'All of them are fine.'

'I've set a small rope ladder down the cliff,' he told her. 'After that we'll go over the rocks to Bell Bay. The tide's starting to come in as we've waited for light. It's safe for half an hour—any longer and we'd have to go up. On this cliff that's not a risk I want to take. I'll wake the youngsters.'

He moved forward quietly, speaking in gentle tones.

The children rubbed and stretched and then threw themselves at him, welcoming him with joyous cries, kisses and hugs. Trudi shivered, trying not to feel the change as Dan threw her sweater back at her after taking it from the girls. He removed his own pack to provide hot drinks and hot wedges of pie. Glenn passed one to Trudi and she took it gratefully. She had the feeling that left to Dan, she might have been ignored. Excitedly the children told him about their adventures. A minute later he had them doing warming exercises to make sure they were completely awake.

He led the way with Robin, then Glenn with Angela and herself bringing up the rear. Trudi, looking at the cliff beside her, marvelled that they had managed to scrabble up to safety.

The sea danced innocently on the rocks, showing the strip of sand in the centre of the Bay in the grey light of dawn. Dan helped the children over the worst rocks and he turned to assist her too. Their hands touched and their eyes met. Trudi saw a hard look shutter Dan's face and felt her heart set up its own protest. She scrambled over the rocks, determined not to need further assistance. With a sigh of relief she saw the waiting vehicle and Anne Forrest, anxiously watching for them. The children ran to their mother's arms. Dan spoke to Dave through the walkie-talkie he wore, and as she walked Trudi heard him give instructions to reel up the rope ladder as the children had reached safety.

Dan drove them back to the Forrests' farmhouse, where the delicious smell of baking wafted towards them. Catching Glenn's eye, Trudi smiled weakly. Despite Glenn's fears, breakfast was a merry affair, but Trudi, sitting miserably beside little Robin, was too aware of Dan watching her to do more than pick at

the mountains of food before her. In an amazingly
short time the children were fed, bathed and tucked
up warmly into bed. Trudi felt a deep weariness, wishing she could do the same.

Mrs Johnson, with a conspiratorial smile at Trudi,
asked Dan to run her home, adding that she would
stay and help Anne tidy away. Trudi felt her shoulders
sag. The thought of being alone with the master of Ti
Kouka was the last thing she wanted. Amid the lavish
praises and thanks of the Forrests, Mrs Johnson and
the children, Dan's attitude to her had been ominous.
He had questioned Glenn quietly and the boy's
answers as he explained about the watch had been
received with apparent understanding. Quite obviously
he didn't blame Glenn.

Trudi looked up at Dan and her heart sank at his
expression. He eased her chair back for her, then led
the way to the jeep, making a mockery of opening the
door for her. Quietly she scrambled on to the high
seat. The seat-belt she fumbled with anxiously, not
wanting Dan to touch her. Her hands were puffy,
scratched and cut, but she ignored the pain, buckling
the belt as Dan climbed in beside her.

The engine revved immediately and they began lurching down on to the drive with scant respect for the
suspension. Trudi risked a side glance at Dan, then
wished she hadn't. By the time Dan pulled up at the
side garage at Ti Kouka, the silence between them was
like a scream.

'What time is it?'

The blank question astonished her, and automatically she glanced at her watch. 'Seven-fifty.'

Dan looked at his own watch in turn. 'Near enough.
One and a half minutes out. Yet you told Glenn that
your watch must have stopped.'

Trudi gasped, realising the simple trap Dan had set. She knew he would never believe her efforts to try to dry her watch. She hadn't even realised it was going until that moment. Again he would never believe that she could have guessed the time with such deadly accuracy. Despairingly she looked up at him. His eyes reminded her of a hunting falcon.

'The others think you're a heroine. You're clever, Trudi, but you don't fool me. You were totally irresponsible.'

His words seemed like bullets fired into her heart. She turned away, but he reached for her, holding her face so she had to meet his eyes. His grip seared.

'You're not welcome on Ti Kouka. I never want to see you again.'

Releasing her, he jumped down from the jeep and strode away. Through a mist of tears Trudi watched him go. Too shocked to protest, she felt his words echoing over and over in her brain. Stumbling, she managed to leave the jeep and let herself in the side entrance. Climbing the stairs was something she could never remember, but she found herself in her own room.

The bed had the covers turned back for her, the blanket was warm. Mrs Johnson had put a vase of tiny rosebuds on the dressing table. The room looked welcoming, and Trudi longed for rest, but after Dan's words she knew she could not stay. Gathering her gear swiftly, she packed her bag and wrote a brief note to Mrs Johnson. She knew carrying the suitcase was impossible, so she asked if the case could be dropped at the flat, or the bus depot, whenever it was convenient. Her watch told her she could catch the bus if she hurried. She sped out the back way, using the track towards the gap.

The grass was wet after the rain of the night and as she ran through the small plantation the branches seemed a barrier. Each time she pushed them, a shower cascaded on her, and by the time she arrived at the creek where she had played so long ago with Maria, she was past caring about the water. She jumped, but miscalculated the distance and her ability to leap, landing heavily up to her knees. Stopping only to remove her water-filled sneakers, she sped on again. She glanced at her watch and made her feet move faster, aghast at how much time had elapsed. Already it was ten to nine and the bus could pass without her.

Fear of the prospect made her pump her knees and when she turned the last corner she glanced anxiously towards the road. At least now she could see the bus as it rolled down the main road.

Collapsing in a gasping heap by the stand of cabbage trees that stood at the fork, she looked towards the road. Her watch still showed ten minutes to nine, and she stared at it disbelievingly. It had stopped, and she could only feel pain at the irony. She had no way of knowing whether the watch had still been moving at the homestead. She guessed her run must have dislodged some tiny droplet. Her bare feet were muddy and she tried to wipe them on some grass. Sanity was beginning to return and she regretted leaving her sneakers on the creek side.

A sound alerted her and she stood up as the bus came into sight. To her intense relief the driver stopped on her signal and she climbed on board. Scrabbling for the money, she leaned tiredly against the bus support, then sank down in one of the nearby seats, grateful few passengers were on board. She shivered despite the heat of the bus and looked back towards the waving flax-like leaves of the cabbage trees, knowing she would never see Ti Kouka again.

Pulling her jacket around her, she stared at the mud streaked on it, then gave up caring about her appearance. Some time she would tell Mr Maugh the jackets made good survival gear, she thought sleepily.

'Lady, wake up, end of the road!'

Reluctantly Trudi surfaced. For a moment she stared owlishly at the bus driver, before her memory returned. She stood up, and the movement made her conscious of aches from one end of her body to the other. Her shoulders felt as if they had been wrenched from the blades and the base of her spine seemed to have twisted itself from the jelly-like limbs which were supposed to support her. She made her way slowly to the taxi waiting by the bus and when the driver pulled up at the flat she could feel only intense relief to be home.

Her clothes had more or less dried on her, though the legs of her jeans were still wet. It was bliss to stand under a hot shower and just let the water steam gently over her. It was too much trouble to do more than wipe off the worst of the water from her hair, before climbing into her bed. With a deep sigh she turned over to sleep.

It took her a moment to realise the telephone was singing insistently beside her and she forced herself awake as she reached for it. Her hair was wet around her face and she knew she hadn't slept long. Groggily she stared at the phone, finally moving her arm woodenly like a string puppet to pick it up. Just as her hand closed around the receiver it stopped. She sank back again and then sat upright, thinking that the call might have been from Ti Kouka. Dan's face seemed to appear before her, promising vengeance. Then she took the telephone off the hook, before shivering her way back among the blankets to sleep.

Trudi woke from her long sleep wondering if the whole affair had been a nightmare. She dressed and made her way to the front door to let the morning sunshine flood the flat.

Immediately she saw the envelope. The letter felt stiff and she knew even before she opened it that it was from Dan's mother. The small neat cabbage tree design etched in one corner of the ivory-coloured paper was artistic as well as appropriate.

'Dear Trudi,

I cannot express my deep regret. I can only guess at the words which must have hurt you so desperately. I beg you not to be too hurt by Sheridan's anger. Because he is my son, I can only ask you to forgive him. In the short time I have known you I realise you have been gifted with a warm, sensitive heart. I'm sorry you must be suffering. I am staying at the flat and I would appreciate a phone call to let me know you are safe.'

Trudi frowned as she read the note again. She should have realised that her hasty flight would cause problems. She dialled the number, and the anxious voice on the other end sighed with patent relief when she spoke.

'I'm sorry, Mrs Johnson,' she apologised, 'I've been asleep.'

'Trudi, you poor girl! What can I say? Thank you for letting me know you're all right. You could have become seriously ill after such an experience. The children are all fine and they send their love. Robin said the next time she sees you she wants you to tell her the pearl story. Apparently she went to sleep in the middle of it and she wants to hear the end from you.'

'Angela and Glenn will be able to finish it,' said Trudi. 'Tell Anne and Dave I'm glad the children are all right.'

'You'll have the chance to speak to them yourself later. Trudi, I know Anne and Dave are full of praise for you. Dave said he doesn't know how you managed to get Robin over the last bit. Trudi, will you come and have some lunch with me at the flat, or if you would rather, I'll take you to town.'

Trudi thought rapidly. She doubted if she could face that hurdle yet. Somehow Dan's anger seemed to have hacked away at her courage.

'Could I possibly leave it for some other time, Mrs Johnson? Since I've been away there's a lot to do.'

The understanding showed in Mrs Johnson's voice as she replied. It only made Trudi's throat feel more full as she replaced the phone. Sadly she knew she could not see Mrs Johnson or the Forrests again. It would be better to try to forget Dan, his family and friends.

CHAPTER TEN

TRUDI flicked her desk calender over. The picture of a sunlit beach caught her eye and she frowned. A month had passed since the disastrous weekend at Ti Kouka.

Her eyes misted as she thought of Dan riding along the tracks, or lurching along the beach road in the four-wheel-drive, or out shifting stock.

Tiredly she reached for the mail the receptionist had just delivered. Flicking quickly through, she recognised the distinctive stationery Maria always used. At least everything seemed to be wonderful with Maria's world, her work was challenging and the new house was offering lots of scope. John and she were having the most tremendous fun chasing the sort of Edwardian furniture the house demanded, and John was wonderful at finding all sorts of little treasures, from old windows to lamps. As she put down the letter the new calendar picture caught her eye again.

'Blast you, Sheridan Jay!'

Trudi felt no better for her outburst. Annoyed, she picked up her clipboard and went along to Rita's office.

'Hello, love, you look as though you picked up five cents and lost a dollar doing so.' Rita's comment made her smile.

'Something like that, I guess.'

'Forget him, love. Other fish in the sea.'

Trudi nodded. There may be others, she thought, but never one like Dan.

'It might take a little time,' commented Rita, her

eyes gentle. 'I thought I'd never love anyone after Mac, and for years I told myself that. Stupid really, I'd shut myself off, and Alf had always been shy; it needed you to push us together a few times to see the joy we could share.'

'You mean you . . .?' Trudi suddenly realised her matchmaking had worked.

'Are getting married? Yes. We're still getting used to the idea ourselves.'

'That's marvellous news, Rita, I'm truly pleased for both of you, and the children. When's the big day?'

'We're not quite sure. Alf and I have been wondering about it. Alf wants to get the designs for the next season in hand and take me off overseas.'

'Right!' Trudi checked her diary. 'You can go on the twenty-fourth and your first stop will be Sydney, to finalise next season's contracts,' she smiled cheekily. 'I give you my blessing to make the negotiations as protracted as you like. If Mr Maugh wants to fly over to Italy, Paris, London and New York to view the latest designs, he'll need someone like you to help.'

'Sounds great!' grinned Rita.

'Your eldest's at university, isn't he? If you go then he'll be home with the first term break for three weeks. Could you get someone after that?'

'You know, it might be possible. I'm sure my sister would stay for another three weeks,' put in Rita thoughtfully.

Seeing Rita's face light, Trudi found herself smiling too.

'Next, what type of ceremony?'

'We'd just thought of a few friends and the family at my local church. I'd hate a big wedding.'

'That sounds lovely,' Trudi agreed.

'By the way, apart from the children, no one else

knows,' said Rita. 'Keep it under your hat?'

Trudi nodded. The work buzzer sounded as she studied the figures. Collating them, she paused, and watched the staff in friendly groups chattering like starlings as they made their way out.

With sudden decision she laid down her papers. They could wait until another day. She wanted to look for a gift for Rita and Mr Maugh, and to buy a present for Maria and John.

The next day Trudi sat at her desk checking supplies of a fabric when her secretary came in.

'Miss Carr, Mr Maugh wants your thoughts on this letter.'

'Read it, please,' said Trudi, as she signed three of the letters the girl had prepared. As she listened she could see why the boss wanted her opinion. The letter invited them to take part in a fashion show in order to raise funds for the Handicapped Children's Society. She looked at the date involved and knew that Mr Maugh hoped to be on his honeymoon at that time. Being fair, he had left the decision to her. She knew it would be extra work, but she welcomed it.

'Write back offering all assistance, and give them my name.' She smiled, guessing the secretary's curiosity. Soon the whole staff would start wondering, as Mr Maugh looked more cherubic than ever and Rita was continuously bursting into little snatches of song.

Trudi picked up the papers in front of her and checked through the previous day's figures. Her head began to ache and she pushed her hair back from her face. A walk would fix it, she thought, and her gaze fastened on the beach scene that featured on the calendar. As always it reminded her of Ti Kouka with its diamond-bright water. She thought of Dan swimming out to her on her island. That had been when he told her he loved her.

'Miss Carr, are you all right?' asked her secretary anxiously. 'You look awfully pale.'

'Sorry, I was miles away,' Trudi conceded. 'I'm due at the fabric warehouse in a short time with Mr Maugh, so I'll check the rest this afternoon.'

She gathered up her bag and went along to Mr Maugh's office. Mr Maugh drove expertly to the warehouse and they found the new representative was an excellent salesman. Both Trudi and Mr Maugh liked him immediately. The substantial order must have pleased their new friend, as he suggested lunch at their favourite hotel.

During the meal Mr Maugh commented about his forthcoming marriage. Immediately their host called for champagne and toasted the happy pair, believing Trudi to be the bride. Quietly she corrected him, and he apologised with a graceful turn of phrase. Trudi glanced around the large room, and her breath caught sharply.

Dan was sitting only two tables away, and from the fury and contempt on his face he had evidently heard the toast. Trudi felt his eyes strip her slowly and mercilessly, then he stood up and strode out, evidently not even prepared to sit in the same room with her. Somehow the mistiness in her eyes she put down to choking on the champagne. Her heart thumped madly and she was totally unappreciative of the fine meal before her.

'Trudi, remind me to see the executive manager about the Gold Room while I'm here,' said Mr Maugh. 'Rita suggested it would make a good place for the reception.'

Trudi rejoined the conversation with an effort. 'That's a lovely idea. But it's a popular venue, so dates could be a problem. They have so many functions here.'

Mr Maugh spoke to the waiter, asking him if it was possible to see the manager later. Consequently, after their meal Trudi found herself walking to the Gold Room with the hotelier and Mr Maugh. Having satisfied himself, Mr Maugh accompanied the manager back to his administration area to check times and dates. Trudi was more than happy to wait on her own in the quiet richly furnished room, until Mr Maugh returned. She did not dare to think of Dan.

The gold velvet curtains caught her eye with their gracious looped style. Two curtains had not been caught back, and Trudi felt an impish desire to hide behind one like a child. She went up to investigate what was behind them. Stepping between them, she could see a small entrance hall leading to a concealed service door.

'In here, Mr Johnson, I'm sure you'll find it most suitable for your function.' A waiter's voice spoke as the outer door opened.

Trudi stiffened, not daring to breathe. She realised her presence behind the curtain was not known and she guessed that so long as she stood still no one would know.

'It looks fine.' The voice was achingly familiar, deep and with a warm lilt. 'How many could it hold?'

'The executive manager should be available and he can tell you all the details.'

Trudi could not hear Dan's reply, but the soft thud of the door reassured her that they had departed to meet the man in question. Thankful that she had not had another explosive encounter, Trudi pulled back the curtain and stepped out.

'So! It was you. I thought I recognised the ankles. I

hear you've hooked one golden fish. I suppose I should congratulate you.' His voice grated.

'Stop it, Dan! You're wrong,' she pleaded.

'I was, wasn't I?' He looked at her, his face drawn and hard. 'Circe enticing me on the beach, as cold and treacherous as the limestone rocks.' He walked up to her, studying her face as though to imprint it on his memory.

Trudi stood quietly under his gaze, determined not to show the feelings that raced through her. Almost idly he stroked the lobe of her ear, delicately moving the finger of his hand around the curve of her neck, and she drew a sudden shuddering breath at his touch. Her mouth felt dry and parched and she moistened her lips slowly with her tongue, a nervous movement he followed with his eyes.

'So you have some feelings, my nereid?'

Instinctively, knowing she could not handle his presence any longer, she backed away. His hand moved quickly to hold her and she stood still, knowing that to flee was impossible.

'A kiss from the bride is traditional, isn't it?' Dan remarked silkily, his eyes holding hers, burning her with their fire, then his arms pulled her closer.

Trudi had meant to remain perfectly still, knowing she was unable to stop him kissing her. His mouth took hers insultingly, and she was aware of the remembered tang of his aftershave, before she attempted to pull away. Instinctively his grip tightened and the kiss deepened. Despairingly she felt her own unconscious response, as her whole body trembled and her arms wound around him. The familiar joy of being in his arms, and the lean hardness of his body, intoxicated her as her pulses leapt and danced. The room seemed to spin round them, as if they were reliving an earlier moment at Seal Bay. She could feel Dan's anger and hurt being replaced by doubt. She pulled her head away to hide her tears, but his hands forced her chin up. Agonised, she looked at him, meeting the questions in his gaze. Hope flared in her as she knew he wanted to believe what his senses had told him.

'I'm not marrying my boss. You had the wrong idea,' she whispered huskily.

On his face she could see the desire warring with his hurt. Releasing her, he stepped back as though her physical nearness clouded his judgment.

'My mother told me you were mistaken about my name. True?'

Trudi nodded, and saw the light of the knowledge flood through him.

'I want to believe you,' he muttered.

'Oh, Dan, you can trust me. I wouldn't lie.'

The door opened and Mr Maugh walked in, his face beaming.

'All fixed, Trudi. The twenty-fourth, as you suggested. A small wedding reception for fifteen.'

Trudi saw the words nail themselves into Dan. He seemed to reel for a moment, then he turned and looked back at her with a disgust, before he walked from the room.

Trudi knew he would never believe her again. Mr Maugh's words could hardly be more innocent, yet more damning, after her plea. Frozen, she followed Mr Maugh out to his car. She spent the afternoon on an emotional boat, swinging first one way and then another as she wondered what she could do. One minute she would convince herself that Dan would hate her more than ever, the next that he still loved her.'

All through the weekend she was unable to decide on the right course of action.

On Monday, Rita and the boss announced their engagement. The factory bubbled with the news. Mr Maugh arranged a giant staff party to be held at his home and as well Trudi organised a small party for their friends, at her own flat. Only then did she wake up to the fact that she had allowed her social life to stop once Dan had left her life. Knowing that she had to improve, she made an effort and found herself enjoying the fun.

Another evening she took Glenn and his brother to the movies, and they mentioned the likelihood of their parents' visit on Friday evening, as there was a week-end break. When, on Friday, the bell pealed she was delighted she had done some baking, hoping they would visit her.

'You said wine biscuits were your style!' commented Anne with a smile, as Trudi served an elaborate sherry cream gateau topped with walnuts.

'This was always Maria's favourite and I don't have her to spoil, now she's in Wellington,' she explained.

'You should make this for S. Jay,' enthused Glenn. 'He's nuts about walnuts!' He reached for another slice and Trudi was glad when Angela spoke.

'Hey, that's a smashing watch. Can I have a look, please?' her eyes were round.

Trudi slipped it off her wrist. Her own had been repaired after the ducking at Ti Kouka, but it had prompted Rita and Mr Maugh to give one to her as a thank-you. She explained about the forthcoming wedding to Anne and Dave, and showed them some of the photographs of the party. When the family left Trudi knew they would be late reaching Ti Kouka. She waved them off, feeling torn, wishing she had been able to ask about Dan or to explain her last encounter with him.

The sun appeared only fleetingly for the wedding day, but that didn't dampen the happiness of the occasion. A number of the staff had turned up to watch the ceremony and afterwards the guests were taken to the hotel. Trudi hid her pain as they were shown into the Gold Room. This time the curtains were looped back to allow the waiters access way. The memory of Dan kissing her haunted her.

Rita made a charming bride, and the bridegroom smiled so much on his new family, it made the happiness contagious. Trudi knew the children would miss their mother and she invited them to have tea with her the following day.

At work the next morning Trudi had the factory to run, and that responsibility challenged her. She had prepared carefully and with her friend's assistance the workload was lighter. At lunchtime she slipped home to put a casserole in the oven for Rita's family.

Later in the day she had an appointment with the fashion compere for the charity parade she had agreed to so long before. She had arranged a sample showing and checking the garments through with the models took time, despite assistance from her staff.

In a week they were to have the rehearsal, and she noted the time and place in her schedule with a wry grimace. The Gold Room and the hotel seemed destined to play reminders, she thought sadly. She didn't need them, she knew; the man from Ti Kouka was always in her thoughts.

As Trudi marked off another week she studied her face, feeling dissatisfied. On impulse she rang her hairdresser. Normally she coped with her hair, but suddenly she wanted it cut. Dan had loved to wind strands of it round his fingers; at least if it was short that would be one less memory.

The hairdresser cut it to a curving neckline, and Trudi stared at her new face, unsure whether it suited her or not. He demonstrated ways she could adorn it by clipping it to the side and waving it to the top to form a tiny coronet for gala occasions.

She wished Maria was there to give her an opinion. Once the boss was back she would go to stay with Maria and John for a couple of weeks, then she might take off overseas herself, she mused.

The thought had no doubt been inspired by Rita's excited chatter about travel, she told herself. There was the possibility that if she saw new countries and met new people she would soon be able to erase the constant ache.

In between checking progress of the monthly figures from the new wing, Trudi was busy checking on the mannequin parade. Most of the staff intended supporting the charity with their presence. Their talk reminded Trudi that she had the rehearsal the next day. The compere had outlined the programme, and now she went back to her office to refresh her memory.

Looking at the models at rehearsal, Trudi stood admiring as one after another entered the tiny catwalk that had been built along the conference room in the hotel. She felt disappointed as one of the models was unable to attend and her absence was throwing out the timing.

The compere had worked out a series of dance-like routines which showed off the various garments, but the gaps were obvious. She became aware of the compere staring at her thoughtfully.

'Miss Carr, you can see the problem. You're about the same build as Jenni. Would you mind standing in for her?'

'Why not?' laughed Trudi. 'I always had secret dreams of being a model at one stage. So long as it's only the rehearsal!'

She changed rapidly, and grimaced as the bathing wear reminded her of the beach at Ti Kouka. One of the models threw her the beach ball and she ran on bouncing it to the compere's instructions, turning to throw it to the next model, in time to the music.

At first she was stiff and awkward, but then she reminded herself that it was just for fun and she relaxed and began to enjoy it.

'You're a natural!' said the compere at the end. 'Sorry I was a bit tough on you at times, but I forgot you weren't one of the girls. That's about the highest compliment I could give. I'll know where to come for an extra model in future.'

'No, thanks. I'll stick to my sewing, it's not such hard work!'

Trudi thought of her earlier experience, on the day of the parade. The event was a formal occasion and Trudi had received her official invitation for the supper after the show. Mr Maugh had left a substantial cheque to be given to the society and Trudi held it thoughtfully, before putting it in her bag.

She had decided to wear the sea-green dress, and she studied herself in the glass. The mirror showed her a fairy-like princess with deep, dark eyes. They shadowed even as she realised there was no handsome prince.

Two friends had promised to pick her up on their way to the hotel, and their delighted comments about her appearance comforted her. Their own dresses were beautiful too.

As the usher showed them to the seats in the front

Trudi knew a sudden panic. Seated beside the President of the local Society was a tall, dark-haired man with broad shoulders and a straight back. He glanced up and their eyes met.

'Dan!' she gasped.

'Ah, I see you've met the New Zealand patron of our Society, Miss Carr.' Somehow Trudi found herself sitting beside Dan, the introductions to her friends completed.

'What are you doing here?' she hissed at Dan.

'I might say the same to you. I thought you'd be in Europe. This happens to be a charity I've taken an active part in for some years. Don't worry, I'll be on my best behaviour, Miss Carr. I see you're still using your own name. May I add that you look more of a nereid than ever? Marriage evidently suits you.'

Trudi frowned. She didn't want to have a shouting match with Dan at such a function, but she had to correct him.

'You're quite wrong, Dan Johnson. However, I've no intention of telling you the truth here and now.'

'Cutting your hair doesn't seem to have shorn you of your contradictory habits,' he snapped, sotto voce.

He turned away to address the local president and Trudi looked sickly at the floor, wishing there was some way she could avoid the next hour and a half. The smell of Dan's aftershave, just hinted at as he had touched her hair a moment before, had almost made her cry. His dinner suit made him look more handsome and distinguished than ever. Despairingly she looked up towards the stage and saw one of the backroom assistants signal to her. Puzzled, she excused herself and went to the backstage entrance.

'Trudi, Jenni ate lobster for tea and it's made her violently ill. You'll have to take her place.' The compere was very definite. 'You know the moves, and the routines from the other day. Otherwise we'll have to scrap that presentation and just do it straight, which would be a shame when you're the right size.'

'Can't you get someone else?' she asked.

'Please, for the organisation?'

The thought of parading about in front of the cynical eyes of the man from Ti Kouka was agonising. Trudi had thought sitting beside him was bad, but now she was being asked to do more. She wondered quickly if she could get one of her staff to take her place, but she knew neither had the right measurements, nor knew the movements.

'You'll have to do it, Miss Carr,' put in one of the models. 'Piece of cake for you! We'll help you.'

Trudi nodded slowly. O.K.'

Reluctantly she viewed her first outfit, a skimpy two-piece which left nothing to the imagination. Her eyes stared back angrily, as she imagined Dan's lips curling. He probably would believe she had arranged it on purpose, she thought crossly.

She pulled on the beach jacket and the hairdresser quickly flicked her hair into place. Lining up as the music started in the first set routine, she caught Dan's look of surprise. The thought made her stand proudly and smile as though that was the one thing she wanted to do. The cheer that she received from a large section of the audience was totally partisan, and she guessed the staff were pleased with her appearance.

After her initial beachwear, she paraded in the nightgowns, and the second was a soft flyaway gown similar to the one she had worn at Bell Bay. She saw a shadow pass over Dan's face and his lips narrowed as she walked along the catwalk. After that the remainder of the show was easier. She had no way of knowing what Dan thought, his face was cold and shuttered. After the interval she determined not to look at him again.

When the final number was paraded she stood in a semicircle formed by the models as Dan made a short speech thanking the organisers and the people concerned. He hesitated fractionally before mentioning Maugh's Fashions and then led her forward to receive a special acknowledgment. As his hand touched hers Trudi felt her pulses leap. She hardly noticed the applause she received. Somehow she managed to walk backstage with the other girls to change into her own gear. The thought of being civil and making small talk with the select group afterwards was agonising. She knew she would have to attend or her absence would be noted. Telling herself she need only appear for a short time and then plead fatigue, she slipped into her own gown.

The compere walked along to the Gold Room with her, and Trudi was glad of the escort. Immediately her eyes sought Dan, and she envied the laughing manner in which he spoke to a group. Somone gave her a glass of champagne, then she was greeted by her friends.

'What a charming man, so interested in our work,' commented one.

'I thought he was more interested in Trudi,' put in her friend with a smile. 'You were sensational! It was a very good show.'

'I'm glad it went well,' said Trudi. 'I never realised how physically tiring it would be. It would be easier to do a five-mile run! Now, I think if you don't mind, I'll get a taxi home. I'm really exhausted.'

'I'll take you home, Miss Carr.' The rich voice behind her made her start, and she froze, her mind unable to think quickly enough.

'That won't be necessary,' she spoke quietly. 'I'm sure your guests require your attention.'

She saw Dan's eyes darken, but his arm inexorably turned her back.

'On the contrary. As you're the person who'd done so much for the success of the evening, it's the very least the organisation can do.'

His eyes danced as he dared her to refuse. She said a reluctant 'Goodnight' and allowed herself to be guided out of the room. Once they were in the safety of the car she turned on him.

'You're insufferable, Dan Johnson!'

'Careful, nereid, I don't like insults, remember.'

In stony silence she fumed as he eased the powerful car forward. Fog lay thickly over the city and he was forced to drive cautiously. Busy with her own thoughts, Trudi took a few moments to realise they were not heading towards the flat.

'You said you'd take me home!' she said angrily.

'Indeed I will,' he answered cryptically. As the car swung up the hill she could feel her emotion building up. He was taking her home, but it was not to her home. In silence she sat beside him, wondering what further torture was in store. All too soon they reached the town house and he ushered her inside, his grip as firm as ever.

'Is your mother here?' Trudi asked.

'No.' The monosyllable was scarcely encouraging. Dan's silver key glinted in the light and she noticed the same light dancing on the silver cuff links with their familiar motif. She marvelled that she hadn't realised from the beginning that he was the owner of Ti Kouka. Tonight he looked the complete gentleman, there was no trace of the feckless, shiftless character who had hefted rubbish tins at Bell Bay.

'Dan, this must be as hard on you as on me. Please take me home,' she pleaded.

She stood in front of the window, blindly watching as a section of the fog was whipped away by the wind. She had felt it spring up in the car park, she remembered. Defensively she sat down, not wanting to stand so close to Dan. The object was defeated as he sat beside her on the two-seater couch in front of the window. Conscious of him with every part of her, she sat stiffly.

'Trudi, sometimes the whole city is covered by that blanket,' he told her. 'It stops one seeing the city. Reason tells you the city is still there, but it's hard to imagine.'

'I don't feel like a discussion on air pollution in Christchurch, Dan,' she said weakly.

'See, over there the city is quite clear, yet this half is still covered.' His arm encircled her to point it out.

'Dan, please stop this and take me home,' she said, trembling. The touch of his arm on her neck, the proximity of his body, had unnerved her.

'Look Trudi.' Ignoring her words, he turned her to face the scene. Pinpricks of lights showed clearly all over the city. In less than a few minutes the fog had disappeared.

'Our relationship was a little like that, Trudi. We saw each other then things happened to block out and distort our view of each other. I learnt tonight that you were the matchmaker, not the bride for your boss. Your friend is a mine of information about people at the factory, and she thought it very amusing that I should have had you married to Mr Maugh. Trudi, I've had other glimpses. For example, Glenn mentioned that you had a new watch, and that your other one hadn't been the same since Ti Kouka. The tyrant

managed to convince me about the identity switch.
Robin told me about the tractor game and I had another look at that cliff. Obviously you hadn't planned
the incident.' He paused and looked at her, studying
her face. 'There's probably a reason for the cheque
and the episode that started this off.'

Weakly Trudi nodded. 'A pin.'

Dan's eyebrows quivered. 'A simple pin?'

'In the packaging of Mr Maugh's new shirt. He went
upstairs to change. I was downstairs making coffee.
Then we went over lighting plans.'

'And the cheque?'

'Three months' wages as a bonus for all the work on
the new wing.'

'Darling, I'm sorry. I'm not very good with apolo-
gies. I've hurt you very badly, my nereid.' Dan bent
and brushed her mouth with his lips. 'Tonight I was
forced to sit there and watch you, and you were so
serene and courageous. Gradually I pieced it together.
At the interval, after talking to your friends, I knew
just how badly I'd misjudged you. I didn't know how
I managed to get through the rest of the show, and the
supper afterwards. I had the compere keep a check on
you for me, so you couldn't escape. I thought I'd have
to wait till you were back at your flat, but your decision
to get a taxi was a blessing.'

'You said you'd take me home,' she reminded him
mischievously.

Dan smiled, his eyes lit and he gathered her in his
arms. 'Welcome home, my darling.'

Trudi felt her eyes close as his mouth touched hers.
The room seemed to sway around her as her blood
rushed through her body. The feel of his dinner jacket
was reassuringly real. For a long moment the lights of
the city below seemed to meet the stars, as Dan held

her tenderly and their eyes met.

'I love you, Trudi Carr,' he whispered. 'This time I'm not letting anything stop us. In four more days your boss is due back. That will give us time to get the licence, time to get our family and friends together, and time for you to get a dress.' He smiled as he wound his finger in her hair above her ear. 'Just long enough, my nereid.' He dropped a kiss on each eyelid. 'To continue. I'm not accepting any delay on this contract, not fire, not cave-ins, not strikes or lockouts. This is a deal with no conditional clauses, time being of the essence.'

He stood beside her and held out his hand. 'Is it a contract?'

Trudi thought rapidly. Dan seemed to have thought of everything. Even the dress could be made in the time allowed, with the whole factory eager to work on it. Never had she made a contract before without conditions, but she had never been so certain before.

Smiling, she held out her hand. 'We have a contract!'

Harlequin Plus

A WORD ABOUT THE AUTHOR

Rosalie Henaghan began her first book shortly after she interviewed fellow New Zealander and Harlequin Romance author Essie Summers on a radio program. "I've often thought I could write a book," Rosalie innocently commented, and in her kindly way, Essie urged her to try.

Now the author of many books, Rosalie is an expert at making use of events and elements of her own life to enhance her stories. One of her heroines is a teacher – as she herself was trained to be. Broadcasting forms a background for another novel, reflecting Rosalie's former profession as a radio personality.

Sometimes, says the author, her heroines are more capable than their creator! Though Rosalie would love to be an adept knitter, for instance, at least one of her heroines is far better at that activity than Rosalie could ever hope to be. Or, she might send a character in a story out into the garden to weed when her own garden is a mess!

Rosalie believes in observing carefully what is close at hand. She is convinced that a writer should examine his or her own background, and then, she says, "as Essie told me – start writing."

Just what the woman on the go needs!

BOOK MATE

The perfect "mate" for all Harlequin paperbacks
Traveling • Vacationing • At Work • In Bed • Studying
• Cooking • Eating

Perfect size for all standard
paperbacks, this wonderful
invention makes reading a pure
pleasure! Ingenious design holds
paperback
books OPEN
and FLAT so
even wind can't
ruffle pages—
leaves your
hands free to do
other things.
Reinforced,
wipe-clean vinyl-
covered holder flexes to let you
turn pages without undoing the
strap...supports paperbacks so
well, they have the strength of
hardcovers!

Pages turn WITHOUT opening
the strap.

SEE-THROUGH STRAP

Reinforced back stays flat.

Built in bookmark.

BOOK MARK

BACK COVER
HOLDING STRIP

10" x 7¼", opened.
Snaps closed for easy carrying, too.

Available now. Send your name, address, and zip or postal code,
along with a check or money order for just $4.99 + .75 ¢ for
postage & handling (for a total of $5.74) payable to Harlequin
Reader Service to:

Harlequin Reader Service

In U.S.
P.O. Box 22188
Tempe, AZ 85282

In Canada
649 Ontario Street
Stratford, Ont. N5A 6W2

HARLEQUIN CLASSIC LIBRARY

Great old romance classics from our
early publishing lists.

FREE BONUS BOOK

On the following page is a coupon with
which you may order any or all of these titles.
If you order all nine, you will receive a FREE
book—*District Nurse*, a heartwarming classic
romance by Lucy Agnes Hancock.

The fourteenth set
of nine novels in the

HARLEQUIN CLASSIC LIBRARY

Great old favorites...
Harlequin Classic Library
Complete and mail this coupon today!

Harlequin Reader Service

In U.S.A.
1440 South Priest Drive
Tempe, AZ 85281

In Canada
649 Ontario Street
Stratford, Ontario N5A 6W2

Please send me the following novels from the Harlequin Classic Library. I am enclosing my check or money order for $1.50 for each novel ordered, plus 75¢ to cover postage and handling. If I order all nine titles at one time, I will receive a FREE book, *District Nurse,* by Lucy Agnes Hancock.

☐ 118
☐ 119
☐ 120

☐ 121
☐ 122
☐ 123

☐ 124
☐ 125
☐ 126

Number of novels checked @ $1.50 each = $_____

N.Y. and Ariz. residents add appropriate sales tax $_____

Postage and handling $_____.75

TOTAL $_____

I enclose _____
(Please send check or money order. We cannot be responsible for cash sent through the mail.)
Prices subject to change without notice.

Name _____
(Please Print)

Address _____
(Apt. no.)

City _____

State/Prov. _____

Zip/Postal Code _____

Offer expires March 31, 1984

30956000000